TIME FOR COPPERNOB

Denny Mallows

Illustrated by
Philip Bannister

Dedication

This book is dedicated to the memory of my parents. Esther Elizabeth Wilkinson read braille with her eyes and helped produce thousands of books for blind children and adults. George Stanley Wilkinson was the best storyteller. He was kind: tenderhearted.

About the author

Denny Mallows has a passion for stories, especially children's stories. She believes that stories are the best way to describe almost everything that happens. Denny has taught children in London and York and student teachers at York St John University. She lives in York with her husband Richard. They have two children a boy and a girl who have grown up. Denny has found out, since writing this story, that her great grandparents lived in Cumbria and must have known Coppernob.

Text © 2015 Denny Mallows and the Cumbrian Railways Association
Illustrations © 2015 Philip Bannister and the Cumbrian Railways Association

Published by the Cumbrian Railways Association,
104 Durley Avenue, Pinner, Middlesex HA5 1JH
The Association is Registered Charity No 1025436
www.cumbrianrailways.org.uk

Design and layout by Michael Peascod
Printed by The Amadeus Press Ltd, Cleckheaton
ISBN 978-0-9570387-4-5

Contents

Acknowledgments

First of all I must thank all the children and students I have taught for encouraging me to tell stories. In particular I must mention the children at Oaken Grove School, York, for asking me to tell them the story of Coppernob. Many people have helped me in the writing of this book. Railway enthusiasts I have found to be generous with their knowledge, fun loving and full of stories. The people I met in Cumbria could not have been more helpful in telling me about their engine and the explainers at the National Railway Museum met every request with interest and encouragement. I am hugely indebted to Michael Peascod in particular, but also his team at the Cumbrian Railways Association for all their hard work and commitment to publishing my book. I would like to thank Philip Bannister for his bright ideas as well as his beautiful illustrations. Thanks are due to Alan Middleton of the Furness Railway Trust, especially for introducing me to the Cumbrian Railway Association. I would like to thank my friends who have listened and given good advice and my family who are always ready to add their own creative ideas. Very special thanks go to Richard who believed in my story, enjoyed joining in the research and sustained me through the many re-writes.

On behalf of the Cumbrian Railways Association I would like to thank those who have donated specifically to the production of this book. In particular I should like to mention the Cumberland News Group Charitable Foundation for their generous gift.

The Cumbrian Railways Association is the local railway history group for Cumbria and North Lancashire. They publish a wide range of local histories associated with the railways of the County. For membership enquiries and details of our books, please visit our website at www.cumbrianrailways.org.uk.

CUMBRIAN RAILWAYS ASSOCIATION

Chapter 1

Time for Change

LIANA was angry. She was angry with her father and now she was angry with her teacher. Deep inside she was also angry about her mother. Given her hair, which was almost red, you might have imagined that Liana would show her anger but you would be wrong. Liana was extremely good at keeping her feelings to herself. The classroom had steamed up. Liana felt stifled. In just a few minutes the bell would go and she would be out in the longed-for fresh air.

The proper teacher had been off school for a while and there had been one supply teacher after another. Now they had a student, Miss Wells. Everyone liked Miss Wells, including Liana. She looked more like a big sister than a teacher, but she didn't stand any messing about. Out of her huge file she produced some really interesting lessons with lots of different things to do. Since Miss Wells arrived time in school had raced along, that is until lunchtime today. Liana had gone back into the classroom to collect the coffee mug Miss Wells had left on the desk, when she caught sight of her own name in the open file:

'Liana (pronounced Lee-Anna) Lagrange Emerson --------- loner or lonely?'

Was she lonely? Liana didn't think so. Did Miss Wells think she had no friends? She would have really liked a special friend, someone she could trust and share thoughts with. It was not as if she was ever left out of things. There was always someone to be with if she wanted. Before her father changed his job and they moved to York, Liana had a best friend in London. When she first started at her new school, girls in her class had often invited Liana home for tea, especially when they heard about her mother. Somehow she had felt uncomfortable in busy kitchens with mothers cooking or rushing in from work. It wasn't that easy to invite friends home with her either, although her dad would not mind if she did. Perhaps she was a loner? Liana looked it up in her dictionary whilst the afternoon register was being taken and that made her really cross. Just because you don't mind being on your own doesn't mean you prefer not to be with others. Why did people have to try and label you anyway?

'Goodbye,' Liana shouted cheerfully to her friends as she pulled on her coat. Miss Wells must have heard them calling back. It was good to feel the cool air but Liana still felt miserable and anxious. Usually she loved the walk across York after school. She could have gone straight home. She liked The Red House with its tall bay windows and deep red paint, but the three-storey Victorian house was large and empty on your own. Most nights Liana walked to the Museum to meet her dad when he finished work at 6 o'clock. The receptionists, the explainers, in fact just about everyone who worked at the National Railway Museum, knew her father. Liana had to report to the desk when she arrived but she was trusted to wander around for the last quiet hour until they closed.

Liana walked slowly at first, kicking the damp leaves, whilst she tried to decide which route to take to the Museum. Today she decided to walk through Monk Bar and past the shops. She would buy a gingerbread person at Thomas the Bakers to cheer herself up. York, not a huge city, with its centre surrounded by medieval stone walls, feels smaller than it really is. Liana liked the web of narrow streets busy with tourists.

'People come from the ends of the earth to visit our railway collection,' she could hear her dad saying.

At this time of day many people were making their way home or back to hotels. Liana was walking against the flow. A sudden voice made her jump.

'Excuse me pet, could you tell us if this is the right way to Union Terrace Coach Park?'

She knew, and had answered this one often. Many of the tourists she met sounded as if they came from no further away than Newcastle. She liked the sound of the names of the streets in York: Jubbergate, Coppergate, Grape Lane, Whip-Ma-Whop-Ma Gate, The Shambles. She walked on along Goodramgate towards the huge, honey coloured Minster, a towering signpost over York. Lights were already on in some of the shops and inside the walls the city felt welcoming. What would she find in the Museum? She kept a flicker of hope but her strongest feeling was dread.

Thomas the Bakers was almost empty which was unusual. Liana put the white crinkly bag containing just one ginger person in her coat pocket. She usually bought two but today she was not thinking of pleasing her father. He had been so stubborn about Coppernob. He didn't even seem sorry that he was causing her so much embarrassment. She tried so hard to talk to him, to know him better and find out more about herself, but he had clever ways of changing the conversation. It was even more difficult to get his attention now he had stopped telling her stories at bedtime. Her dad had always done that. The coming of the railways was his favourite subject, describing the people and their problems as if he had been there himself. Liana missed the stories and hearing his voice as she relaxed and felt sleepy. He looked after her and gave her anything she needed, but at the same time he kept a distance between them. Liana guessed it was because of her mother, but as he would not talk about her she felt left out of her own story. She had no relatives that she knew of, so there was nobody else to ask. It had been a good idea to meet her father at the Railway Museum as she used the walk home to talk to him and that was worth the hour she had to wait. There was plenty to do in the Museum, but Liana had long since tired of the activities and the truth was that she was not all that keen on trains, except Coppernob.

When she was younger Liana's father would call her 'copper knob' and ruffle her copper coloured hair. He didn't do this so much now but the connection had been made with the engine and Liana usually went to look at her on the turntable, to pass the time until her father was ready to go home. Coppernob had been given her name because of her bright, copper firebox dome. There was something about the reddish-brown engine called Coppernob that made you feel she had a personality. Coppernob looked as if she had survived a hard life. She reminded Liana of a patient old horse put out to rest in a field. Despite being battered and old, her elegant chimney and huge copper dome glinted warmly under the spotlight in the Museum, attracting both children and grown-ups. She deserved her special place in the centre of the turntable. The other engines facing her in a circle gave the old engine a special air of importance, and that had led Liana to write the poem. All the Year 6 children at her school had been asked to write a story or a poem for the infants. How she wished she had chosen something else to write about.

In the Railway Museum Jenny was pleased to be back working on the entrance desk for the last hour, having spent most of the day serving in the gift shop.

'What a day,' Jenny said, sitting down and slipping off her shoes under the desk. An older woman nodded in agreement as she collected her things to leave, but she carried on her conversation from earlier in the day as if Jenny had never been away.

'As I was telling you before, I don't like him. Dr Emerson might be good for the exhibits and the visitors, but he could be more friendly to us.'

'Well, I think he is a good manager,' Jenny replied. 'The Railway Museum is much better for his new ideas. Since Mark Emerson arrived we have been busier than ever. There has never been a more successful summer than the last one.'

The older receptionist walked round the desk to leave but then turned back.

'Maybe the changes are a good thing, Jenny, but I feel sorry for his daughter.

She is so serious. It can't be easy for her living with him on her own. He doesn't smile much does he? It must get boring for her coming to meet him every day. I hope he appreciates her.'

'Shhh,' Jenny started to put her shoes back on, 'I can see Liana coming. At least there is plenty for her to do here whilst she waits.'

When she arrived at the Museum Liana was pleased to see Jenny, the chatty young receptionist, at the Main Entrance desk.

'Have they moved Coppernob?' she asked.

'I'm afraid they might have, Liana. I've not had a chance to look yet so I don't know where they've put her. It seems there are to be some major changes. You'd better go and look.'

A small ray of hope had lingered long enough for Liana to feel the bitterness of disappointment. On the turntable stood the wrong engine. It had the wrong name and was the wrong colour. Coppernob had gone. How would she explain this at school? Liana's poem about Coppernob had not only been chosen to be made into a book, but the infants and their teachers had liked it so much they had planned a trip to the Railway Museum. They wanted to see Coppernob on the turntable and the other engines Liana had used in her poem. She had begged her father to delay this move for a few more days. He had the authority; she felt certain.

'Things are complicated just at the moment,' he had said, but he hadn't explained. If he did not understand how she felt it was because he didn't care enough to listen and find out.

Coppernob was still there in the Great Hall but now she was crammed in between a huge engine, with one side removed to show the workings inside, and two other small engines. You could no longer stand back and see her outline and painted rectangle shapes. The lovely old firebox and her brass number 3 did not seem to shine so much out of the spotlight and the dents and scratches were easier to see. Liana felt sad. Walking round the old engine she looked more closely at the paint and ran her fingers over the numerous holes. At least Coppernob was now touchable. What stories could Coppernob tell, she wondered? Had the old engine been damaged on purpose?

With a cautious look around Liana opened the brown door to the little yellow signal box displayed in the middle of the Great Hall, and slipped inside. She sat down on the dusty floor with her back under the sliding window. Recently, she had taken to spending much of her hour's wait in here. No bigger than a garden shed, the signal box was only used to house a video of signals to be watched through the small window. The door should have been locked. As it wasn't, it made a quiet, peaceful place where she would have space to think. Once inside, sitting with her back to the window, she was unlikely to be seen. She felt the gingerbread person in her pocket but didn't feel hungry any more. She pulled out another crumpled piece of paper. It was her poem. She had tried to show it to her father but now she wouldn't. She had thought about him when she had written it, as he would have understood more than anyone the way she had used the engine's names and the characters she had given them. She read it through again:

COPPERNOB

Engines
When the lights go out and the children go home
The Museum engines all alone,
Come to life and talk in a way
You'd never imagine in the day.

Round in a circle the engines stare
At the turntable they want to share,
That place is saved as it should be
For Coppernob, so all can see.

Butler Henderson
Why they love you Coppernob, I don't know
You're just a rusty heap on show,
I think you must be very old
Your dented firebox long since cold.

Evening Star
Children as they wander round
Many times your holes have found,
They count your wheels you've only four
The rest of us have many more.

City of Truro
Tell us Coppernob, please do
Why all the children stop at you,
You must have many things to say
About the Furness Railway.

Coppernob
I am an old engine that is true
There are so many stories I could tell you,
I've worked in the wind and the rain and the sun
There were many disasters and lots of fun.

So night after night when the crowds have gone
Coppernob tells stories to everyone,
She gets the other engines to have their say
And they re-live adventures until it is day.

Hardwicke
Coppernob, you're damaged on close inspection
But you're the best in the whole collection,
We think you did a brilliant job
That's why we love you, Coppernob.

Liana Emerson

9

Time for Coppernob

Liana screwed up the poem and threw it at the signal box wall with such force it bounced back towards her. She felt the heat of angry tears. She had tried hard to make things right with her father but he had let her down when she needed him. She was always responsible and grown up and no one even noticed. She was still a child. Maybe it was about time she did something unexpected. Perhaps she would run away but that would need careful planning. There was nothing much she could do in an old signal box. She read the numbered labels on the signal levers:

1 INWARD HOME
2 INWARD SHUNT
3 DETONATORS (Fog)
4 DOOR RELEASE ELECTRIC
5 OUTWARD HOME
6 OUTWARD DISTANT

Liana had often wondered whether these signal levers could still be moved. She would never do anything like that. **OUTWARD DISTANT** sounded far enough away so she chose number 6, squeezed and pulled.

Chapter 2

A Friend in Time

ALTHOUGH she was still sitting on the floor of a signal box Liana understood at once that things were different, very different. There was a strange smell, the air was smoky and damp, someone was shouting. As she stood up she could see railway lines reaching out into the distance.

She was looking through a window at the end of a signal box, much bigger than the little yellow signal box in the Museum. What had happened? Liana turned and walked to the open door. Through the door she could see that in the opposite direction, the lines disappeared into a railway station with a black and white roof. Although daytime it was overcast, low clouds hung around, everywhere was dismal. She had no idea where she was.

The shouting was getting louder and more urgent. It was a deep, booming voice calling in such desperation she ran out of the signal box, down a few steps and onto the track before she had really taken in what had happened to her. A powerful, brutish looking man was lying twisted across the rails. His dark hulking appearance made Liana shudder.

'Get over here you stupid girl and untie my boot!'

Liana's fingers felt numb, she had hardly looked at the man's face but now she saw his small, glaring eyes and thin, cruel lips. She felt his huge hand grip her ankle and pull her down. Pain shot through her whole body as her knees hit metal and stones.

'You git this boot off girl or you go under the 11:48 with me d'yer hear?'

Liana heard all right, she could also hear a low, rumbling noise and feel the rails begin to quiver. The lace was in a knot and her nails were short. She put her head down on the track and tried to bite through the filthy lace. An engine whistle blew. The track began beating beneath her even more powerfully than the thumping of her terrified heart.

The lace came in two. Wrenching his foot from his boot with one last bellow of anger, the monster of a man knocked Liana out of his way into the path of the relentlessly oncoming steam train. Bursting into sight through the station, the shrieking engine was upon her, shooting sparks, steam belching. How she managed to fling herself out of the way she didn't know. Stunned, she watched mesmerized as the wheels clattered along the rails just in front of her and rattled off down the long ladder of track into the distance. Before she could collect her thoughts, Liana was hauled to her feet and pushed along a narrow pathway towards the station.

'Stupid wench forgot me dinner 'ave yer? Git it. Run!'

Confused and shaken Liana tried to run. Her knees smarted with pain and she didn't know where she was running to. All she could think of was that by running away from this horrible man, she was also running away from the signal box and any hope of getting out of this nightmare.

That's what this must be, a nightmare. Liana tried pinching herself. She felt the nip and then the sensation of falling. The desperate wish that she would wake up vanished as she hit the cinders, sharp little black stones cutting into her hands and aching knees. This was all too much. She was still in this awful place. She hugged her knees, feeling the hurt of new bruises and grazes. Her tears were of fear and frustration.

'You all right?'

Liana felt a light touch on her shoulder and looked up to see a girl with reddish-gold hair like her own. She was quite small, but her big grey eyes seemed to take in the injuries and distress in a way that made Liana feel she must be older than she looked.

'There was this h-h-horrible m-man ...,' Liana stuttered.

'I know who that'll be,' the girl interrupted. 'That's me dad, foul temper 'specially when he wants his food.'

Liana noticed the girl was carrying a bundle tied up in a knotted cloth.

'I'm on my way now,' said the girl, holding up what was probably a packed lunch in the loosely fastened bag.

'What's your name then?'

'Liana Emerson.'

'Mine's Emily Worthington. Don't go anywhere Liana, I'll be back.'

Emily ran off towards the signal box. Liana examined her knees and picked out cinders from her scraped hands.

Liana tried to collect her thoughts. Things had happened so suddenly. She had been sitting in the little yellow signal box waiting for her dad to finish work. The last thing she remembered was feeling angry and pulling the OUTWARD DISTANT lever. Somehow she had left the Railway Museum and travelled to another signal box in use on a real railway. She looked around. The station looked rather grand. Beneath the black and white roof timbers, tall arched windows spanned the lines. Beyond the station she could see cranes and chimneys dotted along the skyline. Behind her, the other side of a long brick wall, she saw rows of grimy, terraced houses. It could be the present time. There were working steam engines all over the country, she'd visited enough of them, but something was different here. What was Emily wearing? She hadn't noticed. Liana shivered, feeling an icy chill, although a

weak sun was trying to seep through the thinning cloud. Big leaf buds were ready to burst open on a tree by the station. It was autumn at home. Liana was aching everywhere including her stomach. It must be nearly teatime although it appeared to be lunchtime here.

When Emily returned she was smiling.

'You're an angel,' she said, sitting down beside Liana.

Surely this was not what happened when you died, thought Liana. She certainly wasn't in heaven.

'Dad thought you were me. It must be the hair. At least you've saved me a beatin' for one day.'

Liana winced at the thought of that vile man hitting such a frail girl as Emily.

'Come on, I've got some food. Let's go and eat it somewhere safe.'

Liana hobbled behind Emily along the path until they reached a sheltered spot on the opposite side of the tracks to the station. They sat down together.

'Are you new to Barrow-in-Furness? How come I haven't seen you at school?' Emily was undoing another tea towel bundle; she offered Liana a hunk of bread and some cheese.

13

'How did you get here Liana, was it by train?'

The truth would sound totally unbelievable, yet Liana needed Emily to go back to the signal box with her. She was so afraid of meeting her terrifying father again.

'Not exactly,' Liana said, remembering the ginger person. She gave the white paper bag to Emily who was delighted and left her bread to eat it right away. Liana changed the subject.

'When does your dad leave work?'

'Not until about 7 o'clock this evening. Why?'

'I'm not from round here,' said Liana miserably, biting into the bread. 'And I'd really like to go home, only I don't know how to.'

Emily looked puzzled.

'Have you got a good imagination, Emily?'

'I think so.'

Emily listened intently whilst Liana described what had happened to her. She was just about to ask more questions when three children came running down the path.

'We could hear you talkin' to yerself, Emlee Worthin'ton,' the tallest boy shouted, looking straight through Liana.

'I was not. I was talkin' to ...' Emily broke off, looked at Liana and then the children.

'Yer can come back with us if yer like,' piped up the next one down in size, a girl in a worn pinafore smock, dragging a much smaller boy behind her. The little one stared back at them with wide-open eyes, but the others were not waiting for a reply.

'They couldn't see you, could they? You must be a ghost.' Emily seemed quite unperturbed by the thought.

'I talk to my mother,' Emily continued, 'and she's dead. She died of pneumonia just after I was born. I go to her grave up behind the reservoir. I can't see her, but I have a picture of her in my mind. I know her name was Amy, and she is buried in a big square family grave. When things get really bad with my dad and everythin', I sit on a little ledge that goes round her grave and I talk to her.'

'Don't you feel afraid in a dark graveyard on your own?'

'No, it's not like that. The Barrow Cemetery is up on the hill above the houses and so open it's usually really windy up there. Other people visit the graves too. I often see a mother visiting her baby's grave. There are lots of babies buried up there.'

'I am not a ghost, but my mother is dead like yours,' Liana confided. Her name was Beth Lagrange. Lagrange is my middle name. I was quite young when she died, and my father says that I don't remember her. But I do. I don't know where she is buried or much about her really. My dad won't talk about it. I wish I could visit her grave.'

'How did she die?'

14

2 - A Friend in Time

'In a car crash, I think.'

'You use some funny words, Liana. You sound as if you've come from a different country. Do you mean that you think your mother was in an accident with a motor?'

Liana nodded, remembering the train and the accident she almost had.

'Please, Emily, will you help me to get home?'

'I will do my very best to help you,' Emily said, touching Liana's hand but Liana could see the worried look in her eyes.

Emily suddenly leapt to her feet.

'I've got to run back to school or I'm going to be late.'

'I'd like to stay with you. Can I come too?'

'Let's hope nobody else can see you then,' Emily said, helping Liana to get up. Liana was not sure that this was a good idea, but it was better than being left on her own. She tied her hanky round the worst knee, and followed Emily who knew a short cut through a gap in the long brick wall. Across the street facing the wall was a row of terraced houses built with red bricks and grey slate roofs. These houses reminded Liana of smaller versions of her own house, as they had bay windows on the ground floor. Above the front doors were little ornamental brick turrets. The small front gardens had low walls and hedges just like The Red House. They walked uphill past many rows of much smaller red brick houses huddled together, most of them with their front doors straight onto the pavement. At the end of each block they crossed a broader road. Liana saw a horse and cart and a bike but there were no cars.

'You see,' Emily said, 'My dad makes me stay home some Mondays to do the washin', so I can't get into any more trouble or afford to miss any more lessons.'

Liana was becoming more certain that not only had she been hurtled into another place, but also another time.

The fortress-like school was on a rise so they were out of breath by the time they reached the gate. Liana could see cranes towering in the distance, and Emily explained that Barrow-in-Furness was a shipbuilding town by the sea. The bell had only just been rung, so they were in time to join the end of a line of girls as they marched into school, through the entrance marked GIRLS in chiselled stone. Only one other person, a tall boy with a flat cap, seemed to notice Liana. He stared in disbelief as he joined the line of boys at the other end of the playground. The school had classrooms leading off a main hall with cloudy bobble-glass windows that you couldn't see through. Liana's school was a similar design but there the likeness ended. This hall had bare walls except for a big picture of a man with a large moustache and beard. He wore a huge red, fur lined cape fastened with massive tassels over a dark uniform with medals and brass buttons. He held a sword with tassels and on a seat beside him, resting on a cushion with tassels, was a heavy purple and gold crown. Underneath it said, 'God Save King George V'.

Time for Coppernob

The classroom rose in layered steps towards the back with a row of desks and benches on each level. There was a map of the British Isles on the wall and a stencilled text advised that, 'The Fear of the Lord is the Beginning of Wisdom'. There was one other picture on the wall in a heavy black frame. Faded children played in the countryside; underneath it Liana could just make out the words: 'To Everything There Is A Season, And A Time To Every Purpose Under Heaven'.

Liana sat next to Emily near the back on a long bench. The teacher, at the front by a blackboard, stood straight and stiff in a high-necked, white blouse and a long black skirt. She had small round glasses over which she stared at each child, as she called their names from the register. 'Present Miss Pritchard,' the children chanted one after the other as their names were called

2 - A Friend in Time

out. A nasty looking cane lay across the front of the teacher's desk, which looked more like a church pulpit really. Liana felt very conspicuous. Although she was average size in her own class, here she seemed somehow bigger and stronger than the other children. There were iron pipes round the room but there didn't seem to be any heating in this classroom, so she was glad of her coat both to cover her up and to keep warm. The other girls were wearing an assortment of clothes. Some wore smock style dresses, and most of them had long black socks with black boots or shoes. Some of the girls wore pinafores over their dresses; Liana recognised the style.

The school Liana went to in York was built in Victorian times. The whole school had done a project on the Victorians not that long ago. She remembered a visit to Beningbrough Hall and felt sad. They'd had so much fun in the old laundry there, but poor Emily probably had to haul heavy washing from a metal tub every Monday. They had been taught that life was very hard for Victorian people without money, but the school project had been so much fun. Even the caretaker and the school cooks had dressed up as Victorians. For a whole day the teachers had taught them in a strict Victorian way. They had to stand up when spoken to and do strange jerky exercises instead of PE. Miss Pritchard looked like a Victorian but was much more severe than her own teachers had pretended to be. They had called out questions to children who couldn't answer, but it didn't really matter if you were wrong. Only now, did Liana feel the terrible suspense of never knowing when your turn might be, or what the consequences would be if you didn't give the right answer.

'Are you a Victorian?' Liana whispered in Emily's ear.

'Not really, Queen Victoria died in 1901, the year after I was born, then there came Edward Vll. Now, George V is King.' Emily replied so softly and yet the teacher glared at her.

'To whom are you muttering, Emily Worthington?'

Emily stood up but said nothing. Liana stood up too.

'It was my fault, she was talking to me because I ... I ...' Liana stuttered to a stop as Miss Pritchard totally ignored her, told Emily to sit down and continued with her lesson. The other children in the class didn't seem to see Liana either. The boy in a cap had seen her, she was sure. How could it be that some people could see her and others couldn't? Had she somehow slipped back to a time soon after the Victorians? Looking around the dreary classroom Liana noticed the date on the blackboard written in neat curling handwriting, 24th March 1912. She wished she had taken more notice of the time-line in her own classroom, which was so bright and lively compared to this one.

History books were given out and children were chosen to read aloud. Emily read well, and received a nod from Miss Pritchard whose face remained as straight as her back. Some children were not so fortunate. A thin, bedraggled looking girl, sitting the other side of Liana, had lost her page. Miss Pritchard was upon her.

'Lost your place again have you, Ivy Tanner?'

A savage swipe of the cane landed on the desk by Ivy's book, the tip catching her fingers where a nasty red weal started to rise immediately. Liana was shocked at the cruelty. Poor Ivy had such thin arms and rough, hard worked hands. Miss Pritchard turned to walk back down to the front.

'Find your place NOW and READ,' she shouted, through pinched lips and clenched teeth.

Liana lent over and opened the book on the right page. Poor Ivy, fighting back the tears, stumbled over the words. Others who could not read well were made to feel ashamed and look stupid. At Emily's school nothing had changed since the Victorians. When Miss Pritchard declared, 'Class dismissed', Liana, as relieved as any of them, crept out behind Emily.

Wondering what had made her to go into school in the first place, Liana thought again about the signal box and Emily's dad. The scream and thunder of the steam train still seemed to be rumbling through her mind. Emily was ahead, walking through the school gate with the tall boy in a cap Liana thought could see her. She walked behind them for a little way wishing she could hear what they were saying. She was desperate to find out if they could help her find the way back to York and her own time. At last they stopped, turned round and Emily spoke,

'There is a problem getting you back the way you came, Liana, 'cos you daren't pull a signal on a workin' railway.'

Chapter 3

Back in Time

T HIS is George.' Emily introduced the tall boy in the cap to Liana. 'We both want to help you. The trouble is we don't know how to help you, now we know you are …' Emily, always sensitive, hesitated choosing her words, 'outside the ordinary.'

Liana, full of anxiety, understood only too well what Emily was trying to say. What could they do, now they realised that she was not just from a different place but also from another time?

George looked thoughtful. His hands pushed down so deep into his trouser pockets his jacket sleeves bunched at the elbows. Thick black hair curled out from under his soft woollen cap and his gentle grey eyes, like Emily's, were full of concern.

'I think we should go and talk to my grandad,' he said softly.

'I must get the jobs in the house done, and prepare the meal for when my dad and my brother get home, or my life will not be worth livin',' Emily said, looking at George.

'Come to my grandad's house in Chadwick Street as soon as you're done. D'you know where it is? It's about half way down, number 26, I'll take Liana with me, all right?'

Emily looked relieved and gave Liana a quick hug as she turned away.

'It'll be fine, Liana,' she shouted over her shoulder. 'I'll be back, soon as I can.'

Emily disappeared into the gloom. The air felt thick and tasted of smoke. It reminded Liana of cloudy bonfire nights when the smoke from the fires hung about, but the air here was far from still. The clouds were high and moving swiftly. Wisps of smoke swirled around her. Although it was not cold, she once more felt the comfort of her coat. Would she ever get home? They had open fires as well as central heating in The Red House. Liana loved the orange glow the coal made when the fire was lit. She loved it even more at Christmas when they sneaked on logs from an apple tree that had been damaged in a storm. The fire came alive then with flying sparks. The wood-smoke smelt wonderful, but it wasn't allowed because York was supposed to be a smokeless zone. Barrow-in-Furness in 1912 certainly wasn't a smokeless zone.

Liana hurried along the darkening streets trying to keep up with George. Although he seemed to be taller than Emily he was not that much taller than

Liana, yet she just couldn't walk so fast. Her injured knees were throbbing. They headed back downhill towards the station and along the road opposite the long brick wall. She was just going to ask him to slow down a bit when they arrived at 26 Chadwick Street. Liana recognised the houses with bay windows and little turrets above the front doors. George went through the gate and knocked on the front door in a rhythm.

'Listen,' he said, 'I knock five times to Bar-row-in-Fur-ness and then they know it is me.'

George's Grandma Annie opened the door and was so pleased to see him.

'Come in, and your friend. Shut the door, it's starting to get cold.'

'Hello, love,' she said to Liana, who was relieved to know she could at least be seen.

Grandma Annie took her coat and hung it on a hallstand just like the one Liana had at home with hooks, a mirror and a place for umbrellas. Liana was shown into a room on the left in front of the straight, narrow stairs. Grandma Annie went through another door behind it, into what must have been the kitchen. George's grandad had his back to them, lighting a flickering oil lamp in the middle of a round table covered in a heavy, dark green cloth. The room was small but cosy, full of furniture and ornaments, like she imagined all grandparents must have. It reminded Liana of the Victorian parlour in the Castle Museum in York. The cast iron fireplace in the museum was just the same as the one in The Red House, and now she had found another one. Maybe they made lots of them just the same. As soon as Liana walked in the room she had noticed the large photograph of Coppernob on the wall above the fireplace. The engine filled the picture and two men in peaked caps stood on the footplate facing the camera.

'That's Coppernob!' Liana said, walking across to look more closely. She was so pleased to see the familiar engine.

'And that is my Grandad Ted driving her,' said George with obvious pride.

Grandad turned round from lighting the lamp and pointed to the figure on the right.

'That's me. I was fireman Ted Matthews in those days.'

'You did drive the engine though, for years didn't you, Grandad?' George insisted.

'That I did. She's a wonderful old girl. We had many an adventure together, but you know that don't you, Liana?'

Grandad smiled and his clear blue, friendly eyes looked knowingly into Liana's. She was puzzled as she was not sure she knew that much about Coppernob really, and how come George's grandad knew her name?

'It is some time ago now, but I remember the last time you were here with us, don't you? You had the young man with you, Joe we called him.'

Things were confusing enough without trying to sort this out. Liana tried to explain that she didn't know anyone called Joe, but Grandad just shrugged his shoulders.

'You will,' he replied.

Grandma Annie came back into the room with a small bowl of hot water and a cloth. She had noticed Liana's injuries and she wiped the dirty cinders from her stinging palms and knees.

'Looks like you've had difficulties wherever you've been this time. I'll get you both some tea and drippin' toast and then we'll see what we can do, you poor love.'

'Liana wants to get home,' said George, careful not to say anything about different times. 'Can you help us?'

Grandma came in and out with the tea and Grandad looked carefully at both Liana and George. When everyone had their tea and Liana was trying the salty white dripping on her toast, Grandad started to speak.

'There is a time, you know, for every purpose under heaven. Free spirits, like you Liana, change times to fulfil a purpose. First of all you must find out what that purpose is. Once you have completed the task, your reason for being here, you will have no difficulty in finding your way back. Let's start by hearing how you got here, Liana.'

'I started off in an old signal box in a museum where I live and somehow found myself in the signal box here in Barrow-in-Furness', she said.

'The South signal box,' put in George.

The old couple looked at each other knowingly, but sat in silence whilst Liana recounted what had happened to her from the time she arrived in Barrow-in-Furness until George had knocked at their door. Just before she had finished her story Emily arrived and George let her in. She sat down quietly on the floor beside Liana. George explained how strange it had been to see Liana when the other children, and definitely Miss Pritchard, couldn't see her. He already knew Emily but had never spoken to her before. He was, however, curious about Liana and wondered if he could help. When George had finished speaking Liana looked hopefully at Grandad Ted, but it was Grandma Annie who began to speak. She looked at all three children in turn.

'I will tell my story now, and you will see your purpose for coming here, Liana. Ted and I had six babies, we loved them all so much and gave them all the care we could, but children are such poor little mites when it comes to diseases. We lost all our babies and so adopted George's father. Not too long after that our daughter Amy was born. Amy married a cruel, ruthless man whose first wife had died in a mysterious way leavin' a small boy. We tried to talk Amy out of this marriage. She was so young and lovely but she was headstrong and would have her way. Sadly, Amy died too, leavin' a beautiful baby girl called Emily.' Grandma looked at Emily now. 'We wanted so much to have you live with us, but your father would have none of it and took you away to his sister until you were big enough to look after the house for him and his weasel faced son. He threatened to hurt you if we tried to interfere and let you know we were your grandparents. We have tried to

keep watch over you, Emily, but it
has not been easy with your father's
uncontrollable temper. Can you ever
understand and forgive us?'

Emily knelt beside her newly found grandmother and put her
head on her knee. Stroking Emily's copper coloured hair, Grandma told her
how they were trying to judge when she could manage having a secret from
her father. Even then, they could not think how they could get to talk to her.

'You're so like your mother. We have loved you from a distance, but
wanted so much to let you know we were here for you.'

Stifling a tear, Grandad turned to Liana.

'This has been your purpose, you have brought Emily to us and judging
from your story you have probably saved her life too. I'll fetch my old

lantern and we will find your way home.' He smiled at her reassuringly. 'But first I have something to show you.'

Whilst Grandad Ted fetched the lantern, Liana watched Emily and Grandma Annie arranging how and when they could meet again. Emily had to rush, but she took hold of both of Liana's hands.

'Thank you Liana, you have changed my life and I shall never forget you.'

'I shall always remember you,' Liana whispered. With a brief wave Emily had gone.

'Goodbye,' George said, 'you've found me a cousin too, you know.'

'Goodbye George,' said Liana, 'I just hope your help will get me home.'

The wind had blown away the clouds. There was a bright, full moon, so although the street lamps were dim, they did not really need Grandad's shining lantern, which bobbed along at his side. They would need it on the cinder track though Liana shuddered at the thought. She was anxious about going back to the signal box. What if Emily's dad was still there? What if she just didn't go back to York and her own time? What if she went somewhere else? She understood that she could not pull a lever in a real signal box and just standing in the box might not work. Grandad did not seem at all worried. As they walked to the end of Chadwick Street and across the road bridge over the railway, he talked about Coppernob and how she had worked for over fifty years pulling iron ore, slates and passengers too. He told her that Coppernob was now on display in a big glass case at the front of Barrow-in-Furness Station. He was trying to take her mind off her problems and almost succeeded.

'Have you ever noticed the rabbit in the moon, Liana?'

'No, I can see the face on the moon, but I didn't know about a rabbit.'

'Well, the rabbit is upside down with big ears. You have to tip your head over to see him. When I was a boy we looked through our legs, but I can see it without now, which is a good job. You should see him too on a night like tonight. Try it.'

Liana put her head on to her shoulder and looked at the moon. Despite

everything she was pleased to see the shape of the rabbit. She thought that Emily would enjoy being with her newly found grandparents. She wondered about her own family. She knew her father's parents were dead, but what about her mother's family? Could she have grandparents somewhere?

Liana was amazed to see the front of Barrow Central Station. It was huge with a booking hall more like a church. The glass roof she had seen from the signal box arched above a row of station buildings, but most impressive of all, was a large and very beautiful glass conservatory, standing alone, like a Japanese pagoda. It was quite dark but the moon and the tall, elegant station lamps threw shafts of light and shadows across the glass. Grandad took out a bunch of keys and opened the door. There was Coppernob looking so friendly, the large brass number 3 glinting in the strange light.

'Get up there, Liana, stand on the footplate, feel the excitement of standing on the best engine in the world.'

Liana would not dream of climbing on the engines in the Museum, but here she didn't even hesitate. She pulled herself up and put her face on the lovely, old copper firebox. She ran her hands over the shiny metal. Where were the dents? Coppernob seemed much more solid, and she had not seen any holes either.

'Where are the holes?' she asked.

Grandad laughed.

'What holes? This old girl has retired like me but neither of us has fallen to bits yet. Coppernob's controls are simple, Liana, compared with the newer engines. Everything gets more complicated it seems, but it has not been easy to improve on Coppernob's design.'

Grandad lifted his lantern so that the golden light fell on the controls. He showed Liana the regulator.

'I used to pull this lever across to control the steam and make Coppernob speed up and slow down. Now, take hold of the big lever just to your right,' he told her. 'This is the reverser. It was used to change direction. If you want to go back you should try pulling it, Liana.'

Grandad Ted patted her hand as if to say goodbye. As Liana pulled, she felt herself falling and spinning. She clung on tightly to Coppernob's lever until she landed with a thump.

'Ladies and Gentlemen, the Museum will be closing in ten minutes time. The Museum shop will close at five minutes to six.' Liana recognised the familiar 'count-down', as she called it and knew immediately that she was back in the Railway Museum. She was puzzling about the time when she realised that she was actually sitting on Coppernob's footplate. She peeped out and dodged back in as an explainer was showing a few last stragglers the way out. With one final pat of the firebox, Liana carefully and quietly climbed down off Coppernob without being seen. She checked the date and time with the explainer. It was still the same day and only the last hour had passed in the Museum whilst she was away. She was back in time to meet her father. Liana walked past the yellow signal box, which now seemed so small and bright compared with Barrow-in-Furness South signal box. She looked in through the window, the lever was back up as it always was. She would keep away from signal boxes in future, she thought.

Chapter 4

Time and Time Again

T HE football report's finished. What d'you think of it now, Joe?'
Joe Palmer took the piece of paper handed to him by his friend, and
read it aloud holding an imaginary microphone. Most people were on
their way out of the classroom, but they stopped to listen to him.

'On Saturday last, Nearthorpe played Fossby in the York and District Junior
Football League. Midway through the first half there was no score, although
Nearthorpe looked the stronger team with two near misses at the goal.' Joe
paused, put down the paper and gave his audience an irrepressible grin before
going on.

'Then the Fossby left back took the ball full in the face, from point blank
range, and was flat out inside the six yard box.'

Joe had really got his audience now. He brushed back his short blond hair
with his fingers, and continued the running commentary with all the drama of
a well practiced entertainer.

'Despite being in possession of the ball, on the edge of the penalty area
and in a good shooting position, Nearthorpe striker, Joe Palmer, immediately
turned round and passed the ball into touch, so that the stricken defender
could receive attention.'

Joe held his crowd for a brief moment and then carried on.

'He proved that 'fair play' isn't just an empty phrase. Three minutes into the
second half, Palmer scored with a brilliant overhead kick, enough to win the
match 1-0.'

Joe was not always as popular with his teachers as he was with everyone else
but he got away with most crimes, as he was brilliant at excuses. Peter, Joe's
older brother, had made use of Joe's talents on a number of occasions to get
out of PE or games, which he hated. Joe used the computer, and his letter
writing was quick and usually convincing. You had to watch Joe though. Once
when Peter hadn't checked a letter Joe had written, he had handed this to his
PE teacher:

Dear Mr Patterson
Please will you excuse Peter Palmer from PE today
as he has had frequent fluid faeces through a hole in his shoe.
Yours sincerely
Elizabeth Palmer (Mrs)

Peter had not got away with it that time, but Joe just laughed and said that he couldn't spell diarrhoea.

Trains held little fascination for Joe. He left that to his brother Peter and his mum. Joe preferred watching people, well - Manchester United football team to be exact. He loved playing football and most nights he stayed behind after school to practise or play in a match. On match days Mrs Palmer and Peter would turn up to support him and the school team. They were a good team. Most of the players had been friends since nursery, playing football after school as often as they could. They had invented their own 'footy code', and could pass words to and fro as quickly as the ball. This, together with one or two really good players, including Joe, had set them on a winning streak. And it looked as if Nearthorpe might well win the York District Schools' Primary FA Cup this year.

Peter, on the other hand, knew loads about railways. He had started with Thomas the Tank Engine, of course, dragging his family to the National Railway Museum whenever he could. Joe had enjoyed going too when he was smaller and his dad was still with them, although even then he had preferred going to see York City play. His dad lived in Norway now with a new, Norwegian wife so they didn't see him much. Joe kept an eye on the Norwegian Premier League. The Norwegian football team had occasional moments of glory, like beating Brazil, and he wondered if his dad went to see them. One day he was going to play for England. They would hammer Norway 6-0 in the World Cup final!

Meanwhile, Joe was on the bus on his way to the Railway Museum to meet Peter and his mum. He did this quite often in the winter when it was too dark to practise or play out with his friends after school.

Mrs Palmer had talked to a professor at the Museum one day and he asked her why, as she spent so much time there, didn't she become a student and study railways herself, so she did. She had a little room in the Museum to work in and Peter usually joined her after school. Joe took out his Manchester United magazine. He could almost hear Mum say,

'I never begrudge the money spent on railway magazines for Peter or football magazines for Joe, as the pair of them read and re-read every word and scrutinise every picture.'

It was true, with a bag of sweets and a magazine in hand, football usually kept Joe happy on the bus and in the Museum until it closed. By that time they were all starving hungry, so they often called in for a pizza or a burger in York on the way home. Joe liked that.

Joe quite liked the last hour in the Museum. He watched the remaining visitors making sure they hadn't missed anything before leaving. The explainers meanwhile, still chatting away, walked people in the direction of the exits. Joe found a good bench and had just settled down with his magazine, when a cheeky little boy ran up and started the video opposite his seat, before running away again and pulling a face. Joe moved off and tried the door of the little yellow signal box. It opened and as no one was about he slipped in and stretched out on the floor. He was soon lost in 'The 10 Greatest United Goals of All Time'.

It was only two days before the infants' visit to the Railway Museum when Liana plucked up enough courage to stay behind after school, and talk to Miss Wells, the student teacher. She was really friendly.

'I know something is bothering you, Liana. What can I do to help?'

'Coppernob has been moved off the turntable, and my poem for the infants won't make any sense now.'

'Don't worry, Liana', she said, 'We will sort it out straight away.'

With that she marched off down to the infants. Liana almost had to run to keep up. There was another student teacher, Miss Thompson, in Key Stage One. Miss Wells went to her classroom and called her by her first name.

'Suzanne, we have a problem with the Coppernob poem.'

Miss Thompson listened carefully, whilst Liana explained again about the engines being moved around, and then Miss Thompson came up with a good idea.

'I'll just tell them that Coppernob has moved off the turntable so that the other engines can tell their stories. It won't spoil your poem, Liana.'

The next day a note arrived, delivered by two infants holding hands. Miss Wells gave it to Liana to read:

'The new story has gone down well, although one of the children in my class has written that the trains sit on a 'taking turns table'.'

29

Miss Wells smiled at Liana and confided,

'The little ones are lovely, but I'd rather not teach them.'

Following her amazing visit to Barrow-in-Furness, Liana had a great deal to think about. Emily was never far from her thoughts. It seemed so strange to have a friend, who had lived so long ago, yet seemed so alive and real. Liana felt guilty about her own anger when Emily was so accepting of all her problems. Liana's dreadful experience with Emily's father was not disappearing as quickly as the grazes or even the bruises. Sometimes, just as she fell asleep or just as she woke up, Liana could see and feel the train hurtling towards her. One night she had shouted out,

'Get off the line. Get off the line,' so loudly she had not only woken herself, but her father had come running in to see what was wrong. She managed to avoid any explanation the next day by saying she couldn't remember what she was dreaming, but her father seemed to be as worried about her as she was about him.

There must be a reason why her father was so secretive about her mother. She understood that he was upset, but her mother had been dead for a long time now. She really needed to know about it. Perhaps her mother wasn't really dead; perhaps she had just gone off and left them? No, surely that couldn't be true, yet there was something her father wasn't telling her. At least Emily had found her grandparents and could visit their friendly home. Might she be able to find grandparents of her own? Liana tried to make The Red House feel more comfortable. As the weather turned cooler she persuaded her father to light a real fire and once, when they were sitting together toasting crumpets, she had almost asked him to tell her more about her mother. She was feeling braver, but something was going on at the Museum that was worrying her father. He was getting even more difficult to talk to.

Jenny wasn't on the desk when Liana arrived at the Museum. She found her eventually, in the Museum shop, unpacking some Thomas the Tank Engine things and displaying them on a shelf.

'Hello Jenny, are you really busy?'

'I can talk whilst I'm doing this. You can hand me things if you like.'

Liana took off her coat and asked right away.

'Can you tell me what's going on? My dad is bothered about something happening in the Museum. If there is a problem with Coppernob, I'd really like to know what it is.'

'I honestly don't know what the problem is, Liana, but you are right about something going on. I can tell you that your father is in a meeting right now with councillors and other officials from Barrow-in-Furness. I expect it is about Coppernob.'

It felt very strange to hear Jenny say Barrow-in-Furness. Liana had never doubted that it was a real place, and had looked it up on a map of England at school. It didn't seem that far from York. It was odd to know what a place was like in the past, but not in the present.

4 - Time and Time Again

With Liana's help Jenny soon had the display finished. They stood back and admired their work together before Jenny returned to the entrance desk, and Liana went through to the Gallery above the Works. She had found a reasonably comfortable stool in front of a video of the Flying Scotsman. She was often there on her own during the last hour. At first she was able to concentrate on things she brought with her to do, but it soon became more and more difficult. On her last visit, when she had started reciting the commentary in her head before it came on, she knew it was time to find a new place. Liana had kept away from the floor of the Great Hall for weeks, except for visiting Coppernob, even then she had walked a long way round to avoid going anyway near the little yellow signal box. Today she felt braver; after all she had squeezed and pulled the lever with some force last time she was in there. She was not going to do that again. She folded her coat to sit on and checked for explainers. Not a soul was around so she opened the door of the little yellow signal box and stepped in.

Immediately, she felt herself falling and her heart lurched with dread at what might be about to happen to her. Liana was furious to find that she had fallen over a pair of dirty grey trainers. They were on the feet of a boy who gave her a cheeky grin as he lifted his head up from a magazine.

'You're not allowed in here,' she said, wishing she hadn't.

'You are allowed, are you?' replied the boy, put out now at being disturbed in his best hiding place yet. They glared at each other, but Liana was shaking.

'Are you OK?' he asked. 'You've gone a funny grey colour.'

'Like your trainers,' Liana was surprised to hear herself point out.

31

Time for Coppernob

Joe almost sang this little rhyme with a big smile on his face:

> 'Have you not noticed, come what may,
> Sure as clouds on a rainy day,
> Everyone's trainers end up grey!
>
> I'm Joe Palmer, trainers a disgrace,
> But better grey trainers than
> A miserable grey face.'

Liana laughed, but mostly with relief at still being in the Museum.

'I'm Liana Emerson, and I'm all right now thanks.'

'That's good, 'cos you looked as though you'd seen a ghost.'

Liana, not wanting to say too much, but not wanting to appear foolish either, tried to explain that she thought she might have pulled the lever as she fell. Joe, misunderstanding completely, began reassuring Liana that signal levers could not be knocked into action. Before Liana could stop him he squeezed and pulled the last lever on the right, Number 6 **OUTWARD DISTANT!**

Chapter 5

Down the Time Line

U NTANGLING herself from Joe, Liana leapt up to see where they might be. They were in a long, narrow signal box, high up off the ground, like a tree house. A bright fire roared in a metal grate and a signalman, unaware of them, was sitting at a desk. He was giving all his attention to writing the date in a big book, and dipping his pen into a pot of ink. Liana watched him write 26th September 1878. Then she stared out of the window, an astonished look on her face.

'Joe, get up and look.' She spoke urgently, staring with disbelief. Joe, dazed and not understanding what on earth had happened, struggled to his feet and stood open-eyed and open-mouthed. There, looking like a jigsaw through the small panes of glass was an amazing sight, Coppernob in full steam.

They staggered out of the signal box and stood, in white early morning sunlight, at the top of a long flight of wooden stairs. It had been raining and the trees and bushes sparkled with silver drops of rain. A thin tissue of autumn mist, rising from the ground, was swept up with the thick white steam, seeping out of Coppernob's wheels and shooting out of her chimney. Two men with their backs to them were concentrating on the front of the engine. One of them, with a huge spanner in his hands, finished what he was doing and stood back, whilst the other held his chin in his hand. The driver pulled himself up on the footplate and tried to ease Coppernob forward. The problem was obvious. Coppernob's wheels were spinning, not gripping the rails at all. Joe walked down the stairs towards the men but Liana stood petrified, remembering Emily's violent dad. The driver seeing Joe, swung down off the engine and Liana watched them talking. The other man, probably the fireman, was shaking his head disapprovingly. Joe waved Liana down. He was smiling and talking excitedly. The driver wiped his hand on his jacket sleeve and shook Liana's hand.

'I'm Ted Matthews,' he said, but there was no need. Liana would have recognised the bright, blue eyes anyway. This was Grandad Ted but he was much, much younger in 1878. It was 1912 on her first visit so Liana worked out that this was thirty-four years earlier. Ted, a young man now, looked nothing like a grandad. Liana introduced herself and began to relax a little. She surveyed the broken metal bars Ted was showing Joe.

'You see,' Ted explained, 'the driver pulls a lever. It opens the sand boxes and lets the sand onto the line to stop the wheels from slippin'. The trouble is I can't mend them here, and this heavy slate train can't make the rise with slippin' wheels.'

Up on the footplate the fireman was muttering.

'Leave them be Ted, no good will come of meddlin' with ghostly beings, on this day of all days, it's not Christian like.'

'Take no notice of Daniel,' Ted smiled, 'he'd be afraid of his own tail if he were a dog.'

Liana looked at herself and Joe. They looked just the same here as in the Museum, nothing like 'ghostly beings', yet to Daniel they must seem less distinct. After all, they had just appeared out of the mist. Daniel had his head down stoking the boiler. Ted and Joe were sprinkling sand on the line. By the time Liana had reached the front of the engine Joe had settled himself up on the wooden beam just behind the buffers. He put his hand in a round hole, the size of a small plate, and pulled out a fist full of sand.

'I'm going to ride this side and throw the sand on the line, you'll have to do the other rail, Liana,' he shouted.

Liana hesitated. It was not that long ago since she had almost been run over by a steam train, but this was Coppernob and if Grandad Ted thought it would be safe, well ... Liana was glad she was wearing trousers but her coat hadn't arrived with her. She had left it in the little yellow signal box. Ted must have been thinking she might be cold, as he appeared with a jacket and a spare driver's cap. Liana put the jacket on and rolled up the sleeves. Ted put the cap on her head and made sure the peak was straight.

'You'd look like a boy if you didn't have so much hair,' Joe laughed. He was clearly going to enjoy himself.

'Climb up on the buffer beam,' Ted told her. Once she was settled, Ted took what looked like a huge bath plug off the sand box on her side so that she could scoop out the sand.

'Coppernob will blow her whistle when it's time to stop throwing. Are you going to be all right?' Ted asked her, but he had no need to wait for an answer. Liana was ready to go.

Coppernob puffed and chuffed, steam hissing and wheels churning. Gradually, as the sand flew onto the track, the wheels gripped and Coppernob pulled the heavy slate trucks with a purposeful, steady rhythm. Liana thought she could hear Joe singing to himself, but Coppernob was making too much noise. They worked carefully, aiming the sand directly on to the lines. Liana was relieved to hear the whistle blow, as her neck was feeling stiff and her arms were beginning to ache. They were being whisked through the country with the sun now rising higher and warmer. As Coppernob pushed her way through the air it brushed their faces like a blustery sea breeze.

'How do you stop sweets slipping down your throat?' Joe shouted across at Liana. When she didn't answer he carried on.

'By gritting your teeth'. It was hard to be serious with Joe.

34

5 - Down the Time Line

'Sing with me, repeat the first line,' Joe called across.
'We sing at football matches when it gets exciting:

> What have we got?
> What have we got?
> Rails as slippy
> As snail snot.
>
> Train full of slate,
> Train full of slate,
> Wheels are sliding
> We mustn't be late.
>
> Sand on the line,
> Sand on the line,
> Sprinkle it down
> All will be fine.
>
> Coppernob go,
> Coppernob go,
> Shiny round firebox
> Starting to glow.
>
> Chickerty chack,
> Chickerty chack,
> How in the world
> Will we ever get back?'

This made Liana remember that Joe had never been here before. She was amazed at how he could calmly sit there singing about not getting back.

'We get back by Coppernob,' she shouted, but Joe had caught sight of the sea and was making up another verse.

Ted took Coppernob into Barrow Docks where Liana and Joe jumped off. They watched as the heavy slate trucks were shunted into a siding, ready for unloading and shipment. They were surprised to see many large sailing ships, covered in tiny flags, anchored in Barrow harbour.

'What are the flags for?' Joe asked, running his fingers through his hair, which was sticking up now anyway.

'Wait a minute whilst I get some cloths,' said Ted, 'I will explain whilst we give Coppernob a polish.'

'Don't touch the reversing lever,' Liana whispered, pointing it out to Joe, 'or our trip might end sooner than you would wish.'

Joe shrugged his shoulders and mouthed, 'OK.' Then he gave her a quizzical look.

'Have you done this before, Liana?'

'Yes, but I came at a different time. Ted was much older'.

Joe smiled, 'That's why you didn't want me in the little yellow signal box.'
Before Liana could explain any further Ted returned with the polishing cloths
and continued his explanation.

'This day, Thursday, 26 September 1878, is a very special day for the town
of Barrow-in-Furness. The Mayor, Mr Schneider, has agreed to make the day
a general holiday.'

'Oh good,' chimed in Joe. 'Are we going to the beach?'

'Everyone will be going to church this morning, but Coppernob and I have
got important work to do first. This morning four churches named after the
Saints Matthew, Mark, Luke and John will all be dedicated at the same time,
11 a.m.'

'Do you really need four new churches?' Liana asked.

'Yes we do. In 1846 when I was born and Coppernob started her working
life, Barrow was not much more than a village with just a couple of dozen
houses, but since then thousands of workers have come into the town from
all over the country. They are looking for work and Barrow needs dockers,
ironworkers and ship builders. The railway too has needed workers. We are
short of houses and schools and we don't have enough churches.'

'What job have you got to do?' Joe asked.

'All the important folk and good souls of Barrow will be goin' to one of the
services. Coppernob and I have had a very special request from the Duke
of Devonshire himself. His Grace wishes to travel into Barrow in his own
special coach pulled by his favourite engine, Coppernob. The first passenger
train on the Furness Railway was pulled by Coppernob. The coach was not
up to much though. It was just an old sheep truck,' Ted laughed. 'She will
be pulling a quite different coach today. Nowadays Coppernob is not used so
much for passengers. She earns her coal and water pulling slates and iron ore,
so it is a special day for her and for me too.'

They all worked hard polishing until Coppernob's deep red-brown paint
glowed and the copper dome sparkled. There was hardly a scratch on
Coppernob given that she had already been working for over thirty years. Ted
stood back to check that Coppernob was ready, but Liana could see that he was
really admiring the engine he loved rather than the polish.

'She polishes up well this old girl,' Ted said, and turning to the children he
added, 'Coppernob has Furness iron ore in her Indian red paint, but not many
people know that.'

With a quick, easy movement he swung himself up on the footplate.

'Jump up on here with me,' Ted said, 'and we will pick up the coaches.'

He held out a hand to help but they were up in no time. Daniel had been
stoking the fire with an enormous shovel and seemed a bit happier. Both
children were far too pleased to be on the footplate to take much notice.
Pulling the reverser, Ted backed Coppernob into a siding where the varnished

teak coaches were shining and ready to be coupled to Coppernob. They clicked and clunked together with quite a different sound to the grinding, noisy clang-clang of the slate trucks banging together. Ted jumped down to check all was well. Joe and Liana followed him to have a closer look at the coaches.

'The first coach is the Duke of Devonshire's private saloon.' Ted told them.

It was taller than the others with solid wheels and arched windows at the front. It looked comfortable with well cushioned, velvet seats divided by armrests. The other coaches had tiny windows and were less well padded, with shiny cloth bench seats. They didn't look at all comfortable.

'The train looks like a row of wild west stage coaches,' Joe whispered.

'Yes,' agreed Liana. 'Like the mail coach in the Museum.'

At the end came a guard's van. The next stop was to pick up the guard at Barrow Strand Station. Liana guessed Barrow Central Station had not been built yet.

The Duke of Devonshire and his friends were to be collected from Cark-in-Cartmel station, close to his home at Holker Hall. With the guard in his van and the engine gushing steam and desperate to go, they set off. Coppernob, as if feeling free once more, raced along.

'Coppernob seems alive,' Joe shouted, 'like a powerful dragon belching flames and bursting with energy.'

'Listen to her chimney bark,' called Ted, 'that's how you tell she's happy.'

You couldn't help but hear the throaty roar and regular whoosh, as the steam shot up into the sky from Coppernob's towering chimney. The big copper firebox gave some protection, but Coppernob's footplate, with no roof and low sides, was open to the wind, which seemed to swirl around them. This made Joe more excited than ever. There was not much space when Daniel fed the boiler with shovels of coal so they kept to the side where they could see the track ahead. News of Coppernob's special train had spread. At each station there were people waving and cheering as she steamed through, whistle blowing. It would be difficult to say who seemed to be enjoying this the most, the waving crowds, the two children, the driver or the engine.

Joe, looking down the line, thought they were heading straight for a rock face. With a breath-taking rush of smoke Coppernob was sucked into a tunnel. The wheels thundered along the track, sparks flew and the firebox glowed red hot in the dark. Ted blew the whistle as Coppernob, billowing steam, emerged into the daylight and pushed on through Lindal, a little country station with people waving from the platform. As Coppernob started to slow, Ted explained that he was picking up other invited guests at Ulverston before arriving at Cark for the Duke of Devonshire's party. An elaborate, arched canopy ran the length of Ulverston Station. On the platform a group of very smartly dressed people were waiting, ready to board. The ladies, in long dresses and wide flowery hats, were helped into the carriages by gentlemen, in long tailcoats and tall black hats. Coppernob was soon on her way again rattling over the bridge across a wide river estuary to Cark.

'Have you noticed that everyone wears a hat?' Liana asked Joe.

'Including you,' he replied.

Liana, had forgotten her driver's cap, it was so comfortable. She looked down at her railwayman's jacket and dirty hands.

'I'm so glad they can't see me.'

They both laughed.

At Cark station a tall, distinguished, elderly gentleman walked away from the small gathering of refined people getting into the Duke's coach. He patted Coppernob as he might a favourite horse. Ted jumped down onto the platform. Coppernob waited, quietly simmering.

'Good morning, Ted. I am pleased to see Coppernob looking in such fine fettle.'

'Good morning, yer Grace. 'Tis a beautiful day for the season.'

'Yes it is, an auspicious start to our most important day, don't you think?' The Duke gave Ted a brief smile, but his eyes were on Coppernob.

'I most certainly do your Grace.'

Ted, following the Duke's gaze, stood very straight by the side of his gleaming engine and Joe and Liana shared his feeling of pride. The guard stood equally straight holding open the Duke's carriage door. By the time the Duke had taken his seat and the guard had shut the door, Ted had checked the water level in the boiler and was moving the regulator skilfully. He found the exact position that would keep Coppernob happy and raring to go. The guard's whistle blew, his flag waved, and they were off again.

Daniel had climbed into the tender to shovel the coal forward. He worked neatly and quickly. He was just jumping back onto the footplate when a big chunk of coal slid from the top of the pile and slammed on top of his hand. He leapt down onto the footplate but staggered, holding his thumb. Dark red blood came up between his fingers, and Joe quickly helped him to sit on the floor. Liana wrapped her big polishing cloth around his hand as he let out a low groan. There was a huge gash along the length of his thumb. The cloth was not very clean but then Daniel's hands were black with coal dust anyway. Beneath the grime the colour was draining from Daniel's face and his eyes closed.

'Daniel's hurt, I think he might have fainted,' Liana shouted to Ted.

'Make him as comfortable as you can,' Ted replied, 'Coppernob needs more coal, could one of you shovel?'

Joe looked at Liana, who had taken off Daniel's hat and was folding her jacket and putting it behind his head. He knew Liana would want a go at shovelling.

'Shall I go first?' he asked her. Liana nodded and he lifted the long, narrow shovel, which was even heavier than it looked. He opened the little door on the tender. The coal began to pour onto his shovel and Ted opened the firebox door so that Joe could feed in the coal. Joe worked as fast as he could, but it

was a much tougher job than Daniel had made it look. Each time the firebox door was open, the hair-singeing heat shot out making their faces glow red-hot. Liana took over for a few shovelfuls, and then they took turns until Ted said they had shovelled enough.

Coppernob was running along smoothly with a gentle swaying rhythm. Sitting on the floor with Daniel, Liana was out of the draught and closer to the heat from the firebox door. Her eyes were just beginning to close with tiredness, as Coppernob pulled into Barrow Strand Station exactly on time.

The important passengers were helped down from their railway carriages and into the street, where waiting coaches were ready to be pulled to church by patient horses. Liana thought it was a good job they didn't walk far, given the ladies' tiny shoes and their long dresses sweeping on the dirty ground.

The guard, seeing that there was a problem, came running up to help. Daniel managed to say thank you to Liana and Joe before being assisted along the platform and into the station. Liana took off the driver's cap and put it with the jacket.

'Our distinguished passengers will not be returning home by train, so Coppernob has finished for the day.'

The children stayed with Ted and Coppernob whilst the coaches were taken to their shed and uncoupled. There would be work to do cleaning Coppernob but others would do that. Ted didn't want to miss the dedication of his own church and needed to wash first.

'I've got to hurry now. I must not be late to meet my Annie. I shall not forget your kindness and your help. I knew that you must have come for a purpose. When the service is over I will return. If there is anything I can do for you, all you need to do is ask.'

Ted made one last check of Coppernob, swung down and was gone.

'It looks like our purpose was to help one 'nob' pull another 'nob' to church,' said Joe. 'Whatever the purpose, it's the best thing I've done since I went to Wembley with my dad and saw Manchester United beat Chelsea 3-1. What do we do now?'

'We pull the reversing lever and hold on tight,' said Liana, which they did.

They managed to climb off Coppernob just before a group of Museum visitors stopped to admire her.

'You're the best engine here, Coppernob,' Joe said, patting her boiler as the Duke had done. 'Never mind if your "fettle" is not so fine these days. You know Coppernob is not painted the same colour as she used to be, except perhaps behind the wheels.'

'Maybe they forgot to repaint that bit?' Liana suggested.

'You mean like I forget to wash behind my ears? I think whoever did the repainting didn't know that there was iron ore in the Furness Indian red paint.'

Time for Coppernob

They carefully collected Liana's coat and Joe's magazine, unseen, from the little yellow signal box, as the announcer was telling everyone that the Museum would be closing in ten minutes time. There was just enough time to wash off some of the coal dust before Liana went to find her dad and Joe his mum and brother. Later that evening, the Museum cleaner puzzled about the thick black ring of coal dust on one basin in the Ladies and one basin in the Gents. There had been no trains in steam at the Museum that day.

Chapter 6

Time to Look

THE infants at Liana's school had a wonderful trip to the Railway Museum. The whole school enjoyed their assembly about it. The student teacher in the infants, Miss Thompson, told Liana that they had all wanted to draw Coppernob. It was only the excitement of having lunch in a railway carriage that had helped her to drag them away. In the assembly most of the children either read out their writing about Coppernob, or held up a picture. At the end they recited together the last two lines of Liana's poem:

> 'We think you did a brilliant job
> That's why we love you, Coppernob.'

As Liana walked back to her own classroom she decided that it had to be tonight. Coppernob had been moved off the turntable for a reason. It was not just a change of display. Whatever the reason was, tonight she was going to find out what the Museum was planning. She thought about Grandad Ted's words: 'There is a time for every purpose.'

It gave her courage. For the rest of the day Liana spent every spare moment planning what she would do.

'Are you all right, Liana?' Miss Wells asked her. 'You've been miles away.'

Liana smiled.

'Yes, I have. Sorry.' She wondered what funny remark Joe would make if he was there, given that they had not only been miles away but years away too.

Liana phoned the Museum as soon as she arrived home. She left a message for her father so he would know she would not be meeting him. She didn't use his mobile number because speaking to him might spoil her plan. It had been crisp and frosty with a milky sun trying to shine all day, but by four o'clock the sun had given up. Liana put on her scarf and gloves to walk round to the supermarket. The shopping was usually done on a Thursday evening, but there was always money hidden in the kitchen for anything they might have forgotten. Liana took it all with her.

The supermarket was bright and busy, but Liana knew what she wanted and where it was. She was soon through the quick checkout and on her way home. By the time she heard her father's key in the lock everything was just as she wanted it. The fire was blazing and the food was almost ready.

'Is there anything I can do?'

Liana refused his help so he poured himself a drink and sat down at the table. He was pleased with her choice of steak and Liana gave him time to eat and relax. She thought he looked tired, but nothing was going to stop her now. She knew exactly what she was going to say.

'You were going to tell me about the plans for Coppernob,' Liana began.

'Not now, Liana, I've had enough railway talk for one day.'

'But I need to know what is happening to her.'

'Nothing is decided yet. I will tell you when it is.' He picked up the newspaper. Liana knew this to be one of his signals to end the conversation so she spoke quickly.

'Who is going to make the decision and when will that be?'

Dr Emerson looked at his daughter over the top of the newspaper.

'It is all quite complicated. We have been trying to settle the problem before the media get hold of it, but we seem to have reached a deadlock at the moment.'

44

'What do the people of Barrow want to happen to Coppernob?'

'The Barrow Borough Council want her back permanently to display in their pedestrian shopping development,' he replied, turning over the pages of his newspaper.

Liana would be sad to see Coppernob leave the Museum but she knew, perhaps more than anyone, how special Coppernob had been to the people of Barrow for so many years. She had to do something to help them.

'Have you been to Barrow-in-Furness?' Liana asked.

'No, I've been to the Lake District a few times but not to Barrow.'

'Don't you think you should go and talk to the people there?'

'No I don't, I have enough good reasons to keep Coppernob in our care without visiting Barrow.'

'But it might help you to see things from their point of view,' Liana persisted.

'I have no intention of seeing things from their point of view. I am looking at what is best for the preservation of the engine.'

'There are so many engines in the Museum. Is it so important to keep Coppernob here?'

'Yes it is, we have the expertise to care for her in the Museum, and it would be difficult to provide appropriate security in Barrow. There are other reasons too, but I'm not going into them now.'

Liana ignored this attempt to end the conversation and continued.

'How can you be so certain you are right? You shouldn't make this decision without listening to the people of Barrow.' Her voice was rising. She was not keeping to her plan of keeping calm.

'What makes you think that I won't listen to the Barrow Councillors, or that you know enough to tell me what I should do?'

With that Mark Emerson picked up his paper and his drink and walked out of the room.

Liana felt so hot her skin was prickling. She opened the back door and she was glad of the sharp air hitting her face. The moon was doing a much better job than the sun had managed, and was full and bright, casting branch shadows from the winter trees across the lawn. Liana tipped her head to her shoulder to look for the rabbit in the moon. He was there. What would Grandad Ted have wanted for Coppernob? He had helped to save her from being scrapped, over a hundred years ago, so that she would remind generations of Barrow children of the history of the Furness Railway, and the importance of their town. Grandad Ted would want her to go home to Barrow, Liana felt sure.

It was coming up to Christmas and Joe was busy. He had been given a leading role in 'Bethlehem Beat', his School drama production.

'Come on, Joe,' his teacher warned. 'What's the point in having such a good voice if you don't know the words?'

'My feet are cold, Miss, footballers' feet need thick socks and boots, not sandals. Why can't we do it in modern dress? I can sing better in my trainers.'

'The words tell the story so you can't make up your own as you go along,' his teacher replied, ignoring his excuses.

'Perhaps I could hold up a scroll and sing the words off that?'

There was a titter of laughter from the other children. The teacher told him firmly,

'No. Stop thinking about football, Joe. You get one last chance to learn the words by Wednesday.'

For once Joe had been thinking about something else other than football. He wanted to know what had happened to Liana on her first visit to Barrow. He wished they had made an arrangement to meet again. He supposed that they just would, but somehow they just hadn't. He had found her home telephone number in the phone book, but even with his confidence he hesitated to phone a girl. She was a friend and it shouldn't make any difference, but his brother would have a field day teasing him if he found out. Going to Barrow was very important to Joe. He really wanted to know more about Ted and Coppernob. Liana knew some of these things.

Sitting on the bus going to the Museum, Joe was trying to learn the words to the songs in the Christmas play. He wondered what the other passengers would do if he sang them out loud. A girl had started singing on the bus once. It was such an amazing thing to do. Most people had looked out of the window or into a book, anywhere except at the girl. When she sang 'Jingle Bells', two old ladies started to join in and then people had relaxed a bit and smiled.

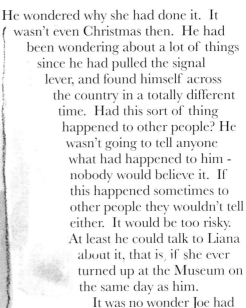

He wondered why she had done it. It wasn't even Christmas then. He had been wondering about a lot of things since he had pulled the signal lever, and found himself across the country in a totally different time. Had this sort of thing happened to other people? He wasn't going to tell anyone what had happened to him - nobody would believe it. If this happened sometimes to other people they wouldn't tell either. It would be too risky. At least he could talk to Liana about it, that is, if she ever turned up at the Museum on the same day as him.

It was no wonder Joe had not met Liana, she had not been to the Museum for over a week. She had avoided going since the disagreement with her father. She had always been the one to say sorry or give him a hug when they had fallen out, but now she was letting him know that she was not going to be the one to back down every time. The trouble was he didn't seem to be bothered that she had stopped meeting him. If she didn't go to the Museum, Liana was never going to find out what was going on with Coppernob. Perhaps, she thought, Joe was wondering where she was too.

It was lonely in The Red House after school. Liana watched the television and played on the computer, but there was still a strange quietness being alone at that time of day. Liana asked two girls in her science group whether they would like to come to her house after school to play. She was pleased at how quickly they had said that they would. They had all enjoyed running around the big house, but what Liana really wanted was to go back to the Museum. Maybe her father thought that she had got fed up of walking to the Museum and was being understanding. Maybe he was glad she was out of the way. She needed a new plan. Liana wandered around the house whilst she tried to get her thoughts straight.

The Red House had a basement. They didn't go down there much, and kept the door locked for security reasons. Liana's friends from school had found the door.

'Where does this door lead to? Can we open it and see?

Time for Coppernob

'Yes, I'll find the key.' Liana opened the door and they went down. The people who had lived there before had started to make it into a flat. It was not entirely underground. From the outside as you climbed the steps to the front door you could see the top of the tall windows. From the inside you could see the bottom of the bushes in the small front garden. The interest her friends had shown in the basement was surprising. Liana had got used to there being just two people in a lot of space. She and her father did not need to use the basement so she hadn't noticed the boxes stored down there before. Locking the door and hiding the key back in its safe place did not stop her wondering what was in them.

The next day after school, she decided to go down into the basement again. It was not so much fun by herself, but she wasn't afraid. The boxes were stored near a window so it was quite light, but she switched the light on nevertheless before she unfolded the lid of one the smaller boxes. Partly, she thought it was all right to look in the boxes, this was her home and she hadn't been told not to. But partly, she felt uncomfortable. These were not her boxes.

She decided to look in one of the boxes just to see what sort of things were inside. There didn't seem to be much of interest at first, just coat hangers and picture frames, but at the bottom was a small tin. She sat down on the floor and pulled off the lid. Inside were old photographs. They were mostly in colour but smaller than usual. There were quite a lot of people she didn't recognise, but she searched through them all looking for the copper coloured hair of her mother. Liana had three special photographs of her mother, taken with Liana when she was a baby. Her favourite one was by her bed. She looked at it so often she felt sure she would recognise her mother's photograph anywhere. There were two photos of her mother with friends, one at the seaside and one sitting round a table at a party. There were two more really interesting photographs. One was of her father and mother together. For the first time Liana realised that she had never seen a picture of them together. The other was her mother with an older man and woman. They all had their arms around each other in a garden with a white, pointed, picket fence. Liana put these two photos in her pocket, closed the box and left. Could she have found a picture of her grandparents, and were they still alive?

Chapter 7

Finding Time

IT was one of those days when concentration at school is difficult. Even Miss Wells had lost her enthusiasm, and several people had been told off even before 'wet play' made matters worse. It was almost lunchtime; water had been spilt, a finger had been trapped in a door and it was raining harder than ever. Liana liked to look out of the window. It helped her clear her thoughts. She watched the big blobs of rain chase each other down to the ledge. They reminded her of the cloudy bobble-glass in the windows at Emily's school, designed so that you couldn't look out.

She needed time to sort out the confusion her life had become. She wanted to be in control. That was a new feeling and a good one. For the first time in her life she knew what it was like to feel powerful. She felt shivers of excitement tingle down her back when she thought about her strange adventures. She wanted to travel back again. She must ask Grandad Ted to help her get Coppernob back to Barrow. With the bell for lunchtime she started on her plan. She told the dinner lady to cross her off the packed lunch list, and she walked out of school with no intention of returning in the afternoon.

A blustery wind whipped the rain, making sure that she was wet long before she reached The Red House. Liana didn't care. She was enjoying the feeling of strength her decision had given her. The weather couldn't stop her now. She knew exactly what she was going to do. She dried her hair and put on a thick sweater before unlocking the basement door. She took her packed lunch with her and made herself comfortable on an old beanbag before unfolding the second cardboard box. It was full of notes and drawings of machines, obviously her father's stuff. In the next box she found her baby toys. She pulled the clattering caterpillar along the floor. It made such a good noise as it rattled around the empty room on the bare boards. Desmond Dog still barked or rather squeaked when she pressed him. She pulled out Pierre Lapin, her favourite floppy blue rabbit. She put Pierre to one side and piled the other things back in the box. Who had given him a French name? It must have been her mother. She knew Lagrange, her mother's name, was French. Perhaps she had grandparents in France?

There was nothing of interest in any of the other boxes except an old camera and a pair of binoculars. There was no more evidence. There were no more clues. Liana folded the lids back and stacked the boxes back as they were. Then she noticed a much smaller box behind the others. Inside were postcards. They were mostly from her Uncle Adrian, her father's friend, who seemed to spend his life travelling around the world sending postcards. At another time she would like to look at the pictures, but not now. Liana sorted the cards methodically. She hadn't realised how much information you could find from a postcard. She started sorting by date to find the oldest ones but the dates were not always easy to see, so she looked at the addresses. Almost all of them were addressed to Dr Emerson but some like Uncle Adrian's included her. She sorted out those to Dr and Mrs Emerson. Uncle Adrian had written to them both so he knew her mother. There were a few just addressed to her mother.

Each of these postcards Liana turned over and over. They were from friends on holiday, with typical messages and no clues. All that is, except one. This one had a postmark from Canada. On the front there were four little pictures and the name NIAGARA-ON-THE-LAKE. The message on the back read:

Hi Beth,
Do you remember our holiday here? It is just the same although
they have Bed and Breakfast now, just like England. Weather
excellent. Food wonderful.
Big hugs for little Liana.
Love, M and D xxx

7 - Finding Time

Could M and D be Mum and Dad? Given the date Liana worked out that she would be two. It was the year before her mother died. Maybe her grandparents lived in Canada? Were they still alive? These two people knew her and sent her hugs. She was going to find out who they were.

Liana took the rabbit Pierre and the postcard back upstairs to her room. She put them safely out of sight, in the box her shoes had come in, at the back of her wardrobe. She was pleased with her afternoon's work. The house felt warmer, the heating had come on and her coat had dried. She put it on and left for the Museum. The rain had stopped but the wet pavements gleamed, bouncing back the lights from the shops. A girl Liana recognised was trying to clean the muddy footprints off the floor in Thomas the Bakers.

'Ginger people,' she called out as Liana tiptoed round the clean bit.

'A pack of four please.' Maybe her order was predictable, but no one would guess who she hoped would be eating them.

'Could you tell me where Mrs Palmer's office is, please?' Liana was glad for once that Jenny wasn't on the Museum desk because she was bound to have asked her why she had not been to meet her father recently. Mrs Palmer's office was easily found. She might have hesitated to knock on the door not that long ago, but not now. Joe's Mum looked pleased to see her.

'Hello, you must be Liana. Come in.'

Liana liked her immediately. She was wearing jeans and a bright stripy top with a zip. She was small and looked younger than Liana had expected. She brushed back her short blonde hair with her fingers and smiled a lot just like Joe.

'This is Peter, Joe's brother.'

Peter was just leaving. He picked up a pad and a few papers from the desk.

'I'm off to the Search Engine. I should finish this bit of research if I'm lucky.' He nodded at Liana, pushed his glasses back up and was gone. He didn't look a bit like Joe or his mother. He was much taller than both of them, with black hair over his eyes that needed pushing back.

'Why don't you sit down for a minute?' Joe's Mum asked.

Liana couldn't see anywhere to sit. There were books, pamphlets and papers everywhere. Mrs Palmer noticed her looking round.

'Oh sorry, just move the things off the chair. I keep meaning to tidy up, but then I wouldn't find anything.'

She laughed and Liana smiled, wondering if their house was this untidy. As Liana moved a pile of books and sat down, Joe's Mum carried on talking.

'I expect Joe to turn up any minute. He intended to play football with his friends after school tonight, but the playing fields will be awash after all this rain.'

Liana had two reasons for coming here. One was to find Joe and the other was to see whether his mother knew anything about Coppernob. She didn't waste any time.

'Do you know anything about the Coppernob problem?'

'Joe has been asking about Coppernob,' his mother replied.

'I wondered why he was interested in an engine after all these years.' Liana tried again.

'Are they thinking of returning Coppernob to Barrow-in-Furness?'

Elizabeth Palmer sat down and looked at Liana.

'You see, Coppernob is a special engine for the Museum and we need her here. The problem is Coppernob is loved by everybody. It is not difficult to understand why the people of Barrow feel she is theirs and want her back where she spent her working life.'

Liana persevered,

'Do you know what is going to happen? Has a decision been made?'

'No, not yet, there is to be a meeting in the New Year. It will be an open meeting so that those who wish to state a case may do so.'

Liana knew at that moment that she would have to make a case for Coppernob to return home to the place she belonged. This would not please her father, Joe's Mum, Jenny or anyone else she knew in York. Even the infants would want her to fight for Coppernob to stay in the Museum.

The door burst open.

'Hi, Liana,' Joe drew his flattened hand across his throat.

'I'd given you up for dead.' Joe did not show the slightest surprise at seeing Liana in his mother's office.

'Hello, Mum. Who wants a jelly baby?' Joe handed round a rather squashed box. Liana chose a green one. Mrs Palmer took two and stood them up on her computer.

'One for Peter and I'll have mine as a reward when I've finished the notes from this book.'

Joe was already heading out of the room.

'Come on, Liana, we've got things to do too.'

Liana said goodbye to Joe's mother and caught him up.

'Where've you been Liana, you've not been here for ages?'

He was heading for the Great Hall and not waiting for an answer.

'I've been thinking about Barrow and I'd really like to know what happened to you when you went the first time.'

Liana too had been desperate to talk about Emily and all the things that had happened to her on her first visit to Barrow. The bench in front of the Eurostar television screen was empty. Before they sat down Joe started the film to hide their conversation.

Liana described everything, trying not to miss any important detail. She had never seen Joe sit still or stay quiet for so long. Liana stood up.

'We have to go back again,' she told him, 'to find evidence to support Coppernob return home to Barrow. I wish there was some way we could control when and where we might arrive.'

'Don't worry about that,' Joe said, as he marched off in the direction of the little yellow signal box. 'I think Ted would say that your purpose would be enough to get you to the right place at the right time.'

Liana could feel the energy of excitement growing inside her. Fear was part of it too, but she wanted so much to see Emily. She felt alive with anticipation. There were children watching the signalling video when they arrived at the yellow signal box.

'You don't want to watch this video,' Joe told them, 'when you could ride on the simulator. It's brilliant. Go to the back of the Japanese bullet train and it's beneath the Gallery. London to Brighton is good but I'd choose Time Travel if I was you.'

'Cheers,' the biggest boy shouted, as he rushed after the others. Liana slipped inside the little yellow signal box and Joe arrived seconds behind. There was not much room for two of them in there. Liana was nearest to signal lever Number 6, **OUTWARD DISTANT** so she squeezed and pulled.

Chapter 8

Railway Time

THEY arrived with a jolt on the floor of quite a big, brick signal box. It was warm and bright with streams of sunlight pouring through rows of windowpanes. The signalman was pushing back levers. As Joe stood up he could see the red tail light of a train pulling into a black and white roofed station. Steam swirled and drifted across a row of arched glass windows over the track.

'This must be the Furness Railway.'

'It's Barrow Central Station,' Liana told him with some relief, 'but we are not in South signal box, we seem to be at the other end of the station.'

'We must be in the North signal box then,' Joe said smiling at her, ready for any experience.

The signalman turned and looked at them both.

'That's right, this is Barrow-in-Furness North, but we recently became part of the London, Midland and Scottish Railway.'

Moving closer to the window, Joe said,

'Hello, I'm Joe Palmer. You have a brilliant view of the station from here.'

'Hello, Joe Palmer,' the signalman smiled at Joe and shook his hand. Looking more closely at Liana, he asked, 'Do you remember me?'

At that moment the telephone rang so Liana was able to look more closely at the signalman whilst he answered it. Liana had known immediately that it was not Emily's father. He still haunted her dreams sometimes. This man was tall but nothing like as big. It was Grandad Ted's grandson, George Matthews. Even with a moustache it was not difficult for Liana to recognise him with his dark, curly hair and soft grey eyes. He looked quite a bit older, but he had changed very little since Liana first met him outside the school. George put down the big black telephone, moved the hands slightly on the big round clock face, and made a few notes in a big register.

'Liana, I'm so glad you have come again,' George said, 'Emily will be so pleased to see you.'

Joe was looking at the equipment.

'Do you use the telephone and the telegraph?'

George loved his job and was pleased to answer Joe.

'The telephone call was our local daily time signal from the inspectors office. All stations on the same circuit check the exact time at 9-00 a.m., the most important job of the day. For our trains to be safe, what matters is that we are

exact to the second and agree. We
synchronize our time with the rest
of the country by telegraph. There
is a saying that not even the sun
itself would argue with railway
time.'

Liana looked in the register. She
was more interested in the date
than the time. She read, 19th
June 1925.

The station was busy. Joe
leant on the window ledge
watching the activity.

'We have a grandstand
view from here. Come
and look, Liana.'

Trains moved in and
out of the station to
a continuous rumble
of sound. Whistles
shrieked, doors slammed,
shunted wagons clattered
and banged together.
Liana was desperate
to ask about Emily
and Ted, but George
was working too
hard to stop and talk.
He worked to a rhythm,
squeezing and pulling
the levers, locking
them in with their sturdy,
metallic clunk and recording everything carefully in the big book. Telegraph
keys tapped and bells rang.

'I'm like a lighthouse keeper up here in my box,' he said. 'My signals make
certain that every train is in the right place at the right time. Signal boxes are
sometimes called the 'lighthouses of the iron road'. There can be no mistakes
with so many people's lives in my hands.'

At last George was able to stop for a moment. He gave Liana a gentle,
concerned smile.

'I expect you have come to see Grandad Ted. He has been ill for some time
now. Emily is very worried about him.'

Liana was sad to hear this.

'How is Emily?' She had thought about Emily so much.

56

8 - Railway Time

'Emily is very well considering that she has just given birth to a beautiful daughter.'

Liana was shocked. It was one thing to see that George had grown older, but Liana found it hard to imagine Emily being a mother. Emily was born in 1900 so she must be twenty-five. George could see the difficulty Liana was having and put his hand on her shoulder.

'It is my baby too. Emily and I are married. She is Emily Matthews now. We live with Grandad in the house you came to in Chadwick Street, all those years ago. Do you remember, it is the road facing the long, brick wall?'

Whilst Liana was trying to understand all this, Joe was asking more questions about signalling and it was clear that he wanted to stay with George.

'Can I still get to Chadwick Street without going through the station?' Liana asked.

'Yes. There is a door in the long brick wall now but you need a key.' He handed her a heavy key bigger than her hand. 'As you can see we value safety these days.'

'I'll follow you later, Liana,' Joe called after her, as she hurried down the stone steps. Liana was soon knocking on the door of 26 Chadwick Street, as it was just the other side of the door in the wall, right behind the signal box. She remembered her first visit and used George's five knocks to Bar-row-in-Fur-ness and waited, feeling a wave of excitement mixed with apprehension.

Emily answered the door with the baby in her arms.

'Liana,' she cried, 'this is wonderful. I'd given up hope that you would ever return. Come in. Come in.'

Stepping into the room Liana was amazed at the difference. The fireplace and some of the furniture was the same, but everywhere was so much lighter and brighter. All round the walls on a shelf above a picture rail were teapots of all different shapes, sizes and colours. The picture of Coppernob with Grandad Ted, however, was still in exactly the same place.

'I was just hanging the nappies out on the line when the baby woke up. Would you hold her for me?'

The baby was handed to Liana who froze, clutching the white woollen bundle as though it might break.

'Don't worry, you won't drop her.'

Liana was not so sure. She could only remember holding a baby once before and that was a big wriggly one. He had almost rolled out of her arms. This baby was tiny like a little doll. Liana had never played with dolls very much so that was no help. She would be very happy to hand the baby back.

'I'll come and take Liana off you now,' Emily said, when the last bit of washing was blowing in the sunshine. What had Emily said? Liana looked puzzled.

57

'We've christened the baby Liana after you.'

Liana looked more closely at the baby in her arms. It was so strange that this little baby would live before her but be named after her. 'We call her Anna most of the time,' Emily told her, 'it pleases Grandad. Grandma was called Annie if you remember?'

Grandma Annie must have died. Liana remembered how kind she had been to her patching her grazed knees.

'Oh look, you've got Anna to sleep.' Emily took the baby and put her gently down in a big tub of a pram, just like one of Coppernob's old coaches.

'How is Grandad Ted?' Liana asked.

'He is very weak and I can't get him to eat much. He sleeps more than the baby. We have a good doctor and we all do what we can for him.'

Emily looked very sad. Liana held out a hand in sympathy. Taking hold of Liana's hand, Emily began to explain what had happened since they last met.

'It was not so long after you came and I met Grandma and Grandad that my life changed completely. In 1914 both my father and my half brother went off to the war; neither of them came back. I would have gone to the hostel for homeless women and girls if you hadn't helped me to find my grandparents. As it was I came to live in this house with them, and I got a job at the steel works. There were all kinds of jobs there for women during the war, but it was heavy work and as you see I didn't grow much bigger or stronger. It was fortunate that I was good at reading and writing so I was given work in the offices. I was lucky. I kept my job until I married George. Other girls had to give up their jobs when the men came back from the war.'

Liana shuddered at the thought of what might happen to her if she didn't have her father. However angry he made her, she loved him and needed him and would have nowhere to go without him. Still, she had come to Barrow for a purpose; to get evidence to fight her father's wish not to return Coppernob to Barrow. She must not lose heart now.

'Is Grandad Ted well enough to talk to me?'

'Oh yes, when he feels well he loves to talk. It is almost always about Coppernob though.'

Emily smiled at Liana.

'You put the kettle on for a cup of tea, and I will see if Grandad is awake.'

Liana went into the kitchen and looked for the kettle. At first she looked for an electric kettle like she had at home. The lights in the house were electric now, but the kettle still went on the gas cooker. She lit the flame with the matches left by the side and the kettle soon made familiar heating up noises. Finding the teapot wasn't a problem but the jar labelled TEA contained loose leaves. Liana was used to teabags. Emily came back in time to make the tea. She liked the idea of little bags with tea in. She used a strainer to stop the leaves from ending up in the tea but a few still floated round on the top of the cup. Grandad was asleep so they had their tea and Liana unwrapped the ginger people. She chose one with a happy face for Emily and took a wonky one for herself. She wrapped up the other two for George and Joe later. The trouble with buying them in a pack was that you couldn't choose their faces. Liana often wondered how Thomas the Baker could give his ginger people so many different personalities, with just two Smarties for their faces. It really pleased Liana to see Emily enjoying the gingerbread again. It was a difficult time for her with Grandad so ill and such a small baby to care for.

'I think we have time for a walk in the sunshine before I need to feed Anna again. Would you like that?'

Liana was happy to have some air although the air here tasted sooty. As they pushed the pram up the hill behind the house Liana could see why. Looking back over the rows of red-brick houses with grey slate roofs, the skyline was dotted with tall chimneys churning out smoke. The higher they climbed, the more chimneys and cranes came in to view. They had passed the school, which Liana remembered well, a church and a reservoir, before Emily stopped at a small shop to buy some flowers.

'The cemetery is just here,' Emily said, 'and I would like to leave the flowers before we go back.'

Liana remembered Emily telling her about visiting her mother's grave but had not imagined such an open, windy place.

The cemetery was on the top of the hill with views as far as the sea. The steam trains puffing in and out of the station were as small as if on a model railway. There were so many flowers on the graves, and despite the warm sunny day, the wind shook the leaves and petals until they shivered. Emily showed Liana the Matthews' grave where her mother and grandmother were buried and she changed the flowers. They tried to speak but the wind carried away their voices, making it difficult to hear. Liana knew at once that Grandad Ted had chosen the inscription, beautifully chiselled in stone:

: BE-YE-KIND-ONE-TO-ANOTHER : TENDERHEARTED :

Chapter 9

Caught in Time

WOULD you like a jelly baby?' Joe offered the squashed box to George when they had a few minutes for a cup of tea.

'We call them peace babies since the war in 1914,' George told him. 'I think they were called unclaimed babies before that.'

'That's a terrible name but good for selling them,' Joe said. 'People must have thought they ought to claim at least a few babies. How could you leave them in the shop?'

George laughed which only encouraged Joe.

'I used to want to be the person who blew the dust off jelly babies, until my gran told me about making Smarties at Rowntrees, then I changed to wanting to be a Smartie polisher. They're made by Nestlé now.' Joe added.

'I've not eaten Smarties. What are they?' George asked.

'They are little, round, chocolate beans, covered with shiny, coloured sugar.'

'They sound wonderful to me.'

'You don't know what you're missing,' Joe told him almost seriously.

Joe worked hard in the signal box. He had never taken much notice of the demonstration electric telegraph in the Museum, but he liked codes. He liked even more the idea that tapping out a beat, or a combination of beats, could make a bell or a gong strike in the next box. He had learnt quite a few by the end of the shift. When Liana called back to the signal box with the key to the door in the wall, Joe couldn't wait to tell her his favourite code, which fortunately they hadn't used.

'Listen to this Liana' he said and he tapped out the code on the desk with a ruler;

2 beats - pause - 5 beats - pause - 5 beats

'This means "Vehicles running away on a wrong line".'

'Why don't you just use the telephone, especially if you had a runaway train?' Liana asked.

'We might do, but the telegraph was here before we had the telephone. The telegraph works well for us and of course it's cheaper.' George told her.

Liana gave Joe and George their ginger people to eat on the way home. George was impressed by the Smarties on the face. By the time they returned to the house, baby Anna was fed and Grandad was awake.

'Please can I hold the baby?' Joe asked Emily as soon as they had been introduced. Emily was a bit surprised, and made him sit down before handing him the milky baby. Liana was impressed as he held Anna so confidently.

'I've got cot loads of cousins,' Joe announced, 'so I'm used to burping babies.'

Liana wanted to go and talk to Grandad about Coppernob, so Emily took her up. Grandad was propped up in bed on a pillow mountain. He looked tired and old, but he still had a brightness in his blue eyes when he saw Liana.

'I was hoping you would visit, Liana. I have a problem I would like you to help me with. You see I'm not able to do anything much any more. These days I drift in and out of the different times in my life. Mostly I'm with Coppernob, reliving the adventures we had together. I had so much strength then. I could spend an hour and a half polishing her beautiful copper dome after shovelling coal all day. I loved that old girl more than the milkman loved his old horse, and he slept in the stable with her when she had a bad cough.'

Grandad shut his eyes and slept peacefully. Liana wondered what the problem was that Grandad wanted their help with. How could she ask him for reasons why the Museum should return Coppernob to Barrow? It did not feel like the right time.

Baby Anna slept too, giving Emily and George time to sit down with Joe and Liana. Together, they all enjoyed the cottage pie Emily had made. Whilst they were eating, Liana explained that she and Joe had been to Barrow again since her first visit, but that they had gone back to a time to when Grandad was much younger and Coppernob was a working engine. George and Emily knew about the dedication of the four churches and the celebrations enjoyed that day, even though it was quite a long time before they were born. It had been such an important day. Liana then told them of her concerns for Coppernob's future, and how she had come to try and get help to return the old engine to Barrow. George thought for a bit and then said,

'I think Grandad wrote a letter once about what should happen to Coppernob. He worked so hard to keep her from the scrap yard, and he wanted to have his views kept for the record. I've no idea where the letter would be now. I'll take Grandad some cottage pie and see if he remembers.'

George returned with the food uneaten.

'Grandad isn't hungry,' he said to Emily, looking concerned, 'and he doesn't seem to remember the letter. He wants to talk to Joe.'

Joe went straight upstairs. Grandad talked to Joe about Coppernob and told him about the problem he would like help with. Joe told Grandad not to worry any more and promised he would help. When Grandad had gone back to sleep, Joe came down to face Liana. He knew she would be anxious to get back to the Museum by now and what he had to tell her would not go down well.

Anna started to whimper. She was ready to be fed again.

'I'll go and see if Grandad wants a drink,' Liana said and Joe went with her.

9 - Caught in Time

Grandad Ted only wanted a sip of water and to talk about Coppernob. They sat together by the side of his bed.

'Did you know that Coppernob arrived in Barrow by sea?' Grandad asked.

'No,' Liana replied, 'Why didn't she come under her own steam?'

'Because there were no tracks. At first the Furness Railway was not connected to any other railway lines, like a toy train set.'

'Did you see her?' Joe asked.

'No, unfortunately, I would have been the same age as baby Anna at the time, but I heard the story told often enough. Coppernob, number 3, must have looked very elegant sailing in to Barrow harbour with her sister engine number 4. They were similar but more powerful than the first two engines numbers 1 and 2. There's only Coppernob left now though.'

Liana was desperate to tell Ted about the meeting and ask him to help her to get Coppernob back to Barrow again. She started to ask

'Grandad, where do you …?'

Grandad Ted had a glazed look in his eye. He had not heard Liana and continued with his story.

'They laid track on the beach and hauled her up on temporary lines to the nearest main line tracks. There were one or two slight mishaps. At one point all those who had come to watch rushed to save her from toppling over into the sand, and Coppernob got known as a character from her first day. Once she was safely on the Furness Railway lines, everyone cheered and patted her.

They fired her up and she sailed more smoothly than the ship she came in. Just imagine how splendid she looked. Glossy new red paint lined out finely in black, brass fittings as brilliant as the dazzling copper dome, every inch gleaming in the sunshine.

Coppernob pulled the first passenger train on the Furness Railway. She was loved by all those who worked with her, travelled behind her or just watched her. Coppernob and I have done our best all our lives. It is time for us both to rest now.'

Grandad sighed, smiled and slipped back in to sleep. He looked so peaceful and happy thinking about Coppernob, Liana knew now that she couldn't worry him with Coppernob's present problems. She went to get him some fresh water. When she returned Joe was looking worried.

'Grandad looks hot and he seems to be saying, 'Anna'. I'll go and get George.'

George came quickly followed by Emily with the baby.

'He is calling to his wife Annie.' George said.

Grandad opened his eyes for the last time, looked gently at them all and said,

'I'm going to my Annie now. People we love may die, but they stay with us for as long as we remember them.'

Liana thought about her own mother and felt sad but these words comforted her many times afterwards. Emily gave Joe the baby to hold and sat on the bed stroking Grandad's hand.

'Shall I rush to get the doctor?' George asked, but Emily, her kind grey eyes brimmed with tears, shook her head.

'It is his time,' she said.

George wept silently but his shoulders shook and tears spilled over his cheekbones. Joe beckoned to Liana and carrying Anna firmly but gently they went downstairs, leaving George and Emily to have the last few minutes on their own with the grandfather they loved so much.

'He was the most caring man you could ever know,' Emily said later as she drew the curtains as a sign of respect.

'He was kind to everyone, tender-hearted.'

Joe tried to think of an easy way to tell Liana what Grandad had told him, but there didn't seem to be one, so he ploughed straight in.

'Coppernob isn't here in Barrow, Liana,' he said, watching the colour drain from her face as she realised their predicament. George and Emily looked puzzled.

'We get back to our own time on Coppernob's footplate,' Joe explained to them. He turned to Liana.

'Grandad Ted has just asked me if we would take Coppernob's sand box lid to London. Coppernob is on show there at the British Empire Exhibition in Wembley. When she was removed from her glass pagoda, outside the station, one of the lids must have come off and got left behind. Grandad does not want anyone to get into trouble for this, and he is worried that the lid might get lost, so the best thing would be for the lid to be replaced without anyone knowing. I told him we would do it.'

Liana lay awake trying to make sense of everything. She had never stayed

9 - Caught in Time

in Barrow for longer than a day before. Would they still return to the Museum at closing time or would they be missing when everyone went home? She knew more about Coppernob now, and Grandad had said things she knew she should remember, but tiredness and sorrow made her eyes sting and blurred her mind.

The next day George had Joe and Liana up with the sun. He gave them a London train timetable and helped them plan their trip to Euston Station. Emily gave Liana a little bag she had made herself; inside was plenty of food to keep them going on their journey.

'Best of luck,' George said. 'Tell Coppernob to come home safely.'

'I will certainly do that,' Liana replied.

Emily and Liana hugged each other, hoping they would meet again. George and Joe shook hands. For a moment all four were silent, sharing their experience but thinking their own thoughts.

Liana and Joe walked quickly up Chadwick Street and across the road bridge to the station, following the route that Liana had taken with Grandad Ted on her first visit to Barrow. They were both anxious to find the sand box lid. Liana noticed that there were now two South signal boxes, and a new path led down to Coppernob's empty glass case. She had forgotten that Joe hadn't seen Coppernob's pagoda shaped conservatory before.

'It's enormous,' Joe said, stopping to take in the towering glass building. 'Even Coppernob must have more than enough space in there.'

Liana was more impressed with the elaborate shape of the windows and the smoothly curving glass panelled roof. She had only seen Coppernob in her case in the moonlight. It had looked beautiful but she hadn't seen it clearly.

'Look at the decoration on each end of the roof. I think the nearest one is a weather vane.' Joe started to run down the slope. 'It makes the double glazed conservatories, they are always trying to sell, look a bit pathetic,' he shouted.

Coppernob's glass building was scrubbed and polished. They both held their breath whilst they tried the door. It opened and they searched inside for the sand box lid. It was not obvious. Right at the back there was a neatly folded cloth. Joe picked it up and underneath was the lid. He curled his fingers round the cool, metal plate and held it up to show Liana with a triumphant grin.

Liana understood that fulfilling his promise to Grandad Ted was very important to Joe.

Chapter 10

Time Travelling

THE station clock showed that they had exactly fifteen minutes to wait for their 9-15 a.m. train to London. Barrow Central Station was busy. The glass panels in the roof cast alternating stripes of light and shade onto the wide platforms, where there were comings and goings of every description. People were pouring into Barrow as other people rushed to pour out. Tickets were bought and ticket barriers squeezed through. There were meetings, partings, people rushing, others waiting. Breakfast was being served and eaten, papers read and luggage transported by hurrying porters. Steam trains arrived, departed and rushed straight through. Goods were collected, delivered, loaded, un-loaded. Men in railway uniforms brushed the platforms, cleaned windows and even raked the gravel. Nobody took the slightest notice of the two children.

'This feels really strange,' Joe said, 'like being in the middle of a film set without a part. I always liked the idea of being invisible but this is weird.'

'I feel as though I really ought to have a ticket. What if the ticket collector can see us?'

Liana was getting anxious again.

'Grandad thought that only the people we need, and those who need us, can see us,' Joe said, trying to make her feel better.

'The ticket collector doesn't need us; he has plenty of other passengers to collect from.'

Joe was pulling a miserable face as he watched a boy his age get a bar of chocolate from a dispensing machine. The machine was underneath an advertisement for Fry's Milk Chocolate. The advertisement showed five pictures of a little boy in a sailor suit. He had short blond hair like Joe only this boy was younger. In the first picture he is crying and in the last picture he is laughing, with a piece of chocolate in his mouth. The middle three pictures show the change, as first he realises he is getting chocolate, and then that it is Fry's chocolate. Needless to say, Joe copied every face perfectly, making Liana laugh.

'I'm sorry you can't have the chocolate for the last face,' she said.

Joe put his hand in his pocket, smiled and pulled out a few large coins. He pushed one of them into the slot and pulled out a metal drawer. A block of chocolate with the five pictures on it was ready to collect, just in time, as their train was announced.

10 - Time Travelling

The engine drew to a halt hissing steam and sending a roll of smoke up into the roof arches. Both children peered through the clearing haze to look at the engine. Liana recognised it straight away.

'Look Joe, it's Hardwicke. Have you seen her in the Museum?'
The tall chimney and big wheels reminded Joe of Coppernob, but this engine was bigger and glossy black.

'It could be Coppernob's big brother,' he said, looking more closely.

'It's not been painted London Midland Scottish red like the coaches, has it?'

'How come you're so knowledgeable all of a sudden?' Liana asked.

They rarely impressed each other with railway knowledge.

'If we're showing off, I know the name of Hardwicke's colour,' she said, 'if I can just remember it.'

'Most people call it black,' Joe said, raising his eyebrows.

'No, its blackcurrant or ...' Liana thought hard, 'blackberry black, that's it.'
Joe started to laugh.

'I know where you've got that from. You've spent your last hour in the Museum watching the film 'Changing Colours'.

'Yes I have. The seats there are comfortable but you can only hear the commentary so many times,' Liana admitted.

'It was the tinky-tonky tunes which drove me out,' Joe confessed. 'You can only hear them so many times too.'

A guard at the far end of the train was slamming the carriage doors shut, so they hurried to get in. It was a through carriage so they walked along the corridor at the side until they found an empty compartment. They slid back the wooden door closing it behind them and sat down. Joe put the sand box lid on the seat.

'Have you any idea how heavy this is?'

Liana shook her head and tried lifting it. She pulled a face and dropped it back onto the seat quickly.

'It is heavy enough to need its own ticket,' she said, impressed that Joe hadn't complained before.

Joe lifted the leather strap off the metal stud and gently lowered the wooden framed window. Whistle answered whistle. Joe watched as flags were waved and Hardwicke shot swirling masses of white steam up into the air. The engine gave a deep, deafening roar followed by first one long chuff then another. Puffing faster and faster the powerful little engine pulled the coaches smoothly out of the station into the morning sun. Smoke seeped into the coach making the children cough. Joe shut the window. The smoke floated above their heads; they watched the wisps curl and disappear.

The start of their journey to Euston followed the same route as Coppernob had taken to collect the Duke of Devonshire. They steamed through Lindal, Ulverston, across the water and on past Cark. Liana thought about Grandad Ted and how much he had loved to drive Copppernob over these same railway lines. In no time they had passed through a pretty station named

Grange-Over-Sands. Once more they crossed a bridge over a wide estuary to the sea, before turning south towards Lancaster, then on to London and the British Empire Exhibition.

The carriage had plush dark red seating. There were no armrests or dividers, but each of the six seats had a number on a little white oval disc. There seemed to be so much brass and someone had been polishing it. Small posters and two mirrors decorated the space between the top of the seats and the knotted luggage racks. The posters were advertisements for places to travel to on the London Midland and Scottish Railway.

'Have you been to Alton Towers?' Joe asked Liana.

She shook her head.

'I've always wanted to go,' Joe continued, 'but now I've seen this poster I'll go in our own time. Look, not an amusement or a ride in sight.'

Brightly painted flowers edged a picture full of towers and terraces with a bandstand and a lake.

'Some things have definitely got better,' Liana agreed.

Joe was getting more and more excited about going to Wembley. He was looking forward to seeing the old Stadium as it used to be with twin white towers. He told Liana his dad and some friends had been several times to the old Wembley Stadium. He knew what it looked like because his friend's dad bought a replica; a perfect scale model of the old stadium. It cost sixty pounds so they were only allowed to look. Liana was tired and happy enough to listen, as Joe went on to give her a kick-by-kick account of the match he saw at the new Wembley Stadium. From Joe's point of view Manchester United should always win; it was just bad luck if they lost.

'Would you like some Five Boys chocolate?' Joe asked. He was trying to break the small bar in half, which was not easy with five pieces. He gave Liana her fair share before taking a few remaining coins out of his pocket and sharing them out too.

'George gave me these old pennies in case we needed them. We can keep them as souvenirs if we don't. My gran has a pot full of old pennies somewhere. We looked through them once because some dates are worth a lot of money, but we didn't have any valuable ones.'

Liana told Joe about wanting to find out if she had grandparents and how there seemed to be some evidence for them being French, yet there seemed to be a Canadian connection too.

'I might have some information to help you with this,' Joe said.

'Only Smarties have the answer. Well, I think it was Smarties although it could have been Fruit Pastilles. Anyway, Canada totally refused to have the sweets because the ingredients were only listed in English and not in French. We might think Canadians speak English, but there must be a lot of people in Canada who speak French. Some people must think that both languages are important, at least when choosing sweets. I think your lost relations are Canadians who speak French, Liana.'

70

10 - Time Travelling

This made a lot of sense and gave her something to think about whilst Joe got out the words for his Christmas Play, and tried to learn them.

'This feels odd practising for Christmas in the middle of summer,' he said. By the time they arrived at Crewe Station they were feeling hungry. Quite a few people walked down the corridor and looked through the windows but no one seemed to want to sit in their compartment. Liana got down the little handmade bag Emily had given her from the knotted luggage rack. There were drinks, sandwiches, apples and two gingerbread men inside. They were different from Thomas the Baker's ginger people, much harder with longer legs and currant buttons. Their eyes were currants but their little red mouths were made from sweets. Joe recognised them. 'I've had those before they're called cherry lips. I had some from the old fashioned sweet shop when my Aunty Jane took us to Beamish Museum. They are probably all right in ones but a mouthful was like eating nail varnish.'

Liana didn't think nail varnish tasted of anything when you bit it off your nails although the smell was a bit like pear drops. She ate the cherry lip in the end and it was all right. She decided to go off for a walk down the train to stretch her legs.

'You just have to visit the loo,' Liana said, when she returned. 'It's more of a throne with a huge wooden seat and a strange patterned basin sunk into a wooden shelf.'

'Historical toilets are not my favourite thing usually but I'll have to go anyway.' Joe jumped up and went to see for himself. The food had re-fuelled him, just like putting coal into Coppernob. Not long after, he slid open the compartment door and put his head in.

'We are in third class here Liana. If this luxury is third class, what is first class like?'

'Shall we go and look?' Liana asked, getting up and joining Joe in the corridor. Liana was definitely getting braver, Joe thought.

They swayed down the train as it bounced and rattled over the uneven track. The dining car was full and people seemed to be enjoying the huge long list of food given on the menu. Wine bottles tinkled in ornate brass holders on the windows; waiters hurried up and down making sure everyone had what they wanted.

The children returned to their carriage and ate their apples. Liana was looking at a menu she had picked up.

'Apples must be healthier than Strawberry Bavarois or Ratafia Pudding whatever they are.' Liana said, not even convincing herself that she wouldn't prefer them. Joe frowned. There was no doubting his sweet tooth. He tugged the leather window strap again so that he could throw out the apple core. In came the now familiar smoky smell and flying black smuts.

Hardwicke, whistle blowing, was rounding a curve in the line and without leaning out too far they could see to both the front and the back of the train. It had been a long journey. It had been different and it had been fun, but now they wanted to get on with whatever was lying ahead.

Euston Station was very busy, but there were signposts everywhere to the Empire Exhibition and the Wembley trains. They joined the crowds, had no trouble at the ticket barriers, and were soon squashed in a coach full of passengers determined to enjoy themselves. A man in a suit with a hat like a gangster was reading a pamphlet to his friends.

'Did you know that there are over fifteen miles of road in the Empire Exhibition grounds?'

It seemed that nobody did know, so he carried on reading.

'It's not only the Stadium that's enormous. It says here that the Palace of Engineering is similar in size and includes the most extensive and comprehensive display of engineering and machinery ever gathered together under one roof.'

A flicker of nervousness ran through Liana. What if they couldn't find Coppernob? No, they had come all this way. They would find her. They must find her.

At first as they hurtled into the countryside, Joe thought that they were going the wrong way, but then he remembered that they had gone back more than eighty five years, when London was less built up. It was hot and stuffy, with little comfort on this bit of the journey, but the train raced along as if it were being chased. At last they slowed down and pulled to a halt, the engine steaming like a racehorse. The children were grateful to spill out onto Wembley Park platform and escape into the sunshine with everyone else. Joe looked round at the ivy covered station under the trees. This was not how he remembered it at all.

Chapter 11

Time's a Thief

KALEEM was just wandering about. He had worked hard all morning cleaning and polishing the Indian Railway exhibits for his father, and now he had time just to please himself. There were so many things to do in the British Empire Exhibition, but it wasn't much fun on your own. He had begged to be allowed to travel with his father to England, but he missed the sisters and brothers, cousins and friends he had left back in India. He wasn't sorry that he had come though. He liked the British weather even the cold and the rain, but a day like today was perfect. He felt the London summer sun as gentle warmth after the fierce heat of his city, Lahore.

There were few people who had visited as many places in the Exhibition as Kaleem. It had taken him many months because the Exhibition was huge. He was always finding yet another building, stand or kiosk he had missed. He had only just found the Hong Kong exhibit because it was right in a corner. He had been back a couple of times to walk along the Chinese Street and eat the strange Chinese food. When it was wet, Kaleem watched films. Nearly all the Overseas Pavilions had picture palaces where the silver screen showed life in that country. Kaleem felt as if he had travelled the world several times without going outside Wembley. It was perhaps because he spent so much time on his own that Kaleem noticed even the little things. The most important thing he had noticed was that the floor of an old railway carriage, in a siding, was filling up with all sorts of different pieces of metal. He had just been interested at first, but then he had seen an Indian brass jug. Even if there had been something wrong with it, he knew that no Indian would have thrown it away. He was suspicious and decided to investigate.

There was definitely something strange going on. Kaleem made himself a den in a clump of bushes beside the railway siding, where he could watch the comings and goings of the people who visited the old carriage. He always kept a small notebook in his pocket to draw and record the things that interested him. Maths and art had always been his best subjects at school. He drew pencil sketches of the men who came to the old carriage. He recorded, with the accuracy of railway time, when they arrived and departed. Odd shaped bundles were brought to the carriage, which he presumed were more metal things, but Kaleem could not always see what was in them.

The plan for today had been to track down where the brass Indian jug had come from. Kaleem sat on the steps of the Indian Pavilion and drew the jug from memory. It would be easy just to show his picture and ask if anyone had lost a jug like this. The sun was warm on his neck as he turned to go back indoors. It tempted Kaleem away from his intentions for the time being. He left the India Pavilion and walked down Circus Avenue towards Exhibition Station. It was then that he saw the two children struggling with a heavy metal disc.

Things were not going as well as expected for Joe and Liana at the British Empire Exhibition. Joe really wanted to retrace his steps down Olympic Way to the Stadium but he couldn't get his bearings. The Exhibition was enormous. There seemed to be so many tall buildings and trees in the way. Liana wanted to get on the 'Never-Stop Railway' like most of the other passengers from their train, but neither of them knew if this would take them nearer or farther from Coppernob.

'This is worse than when visitors to York can't find their coach park and their bus is due to leave,' Liana moaned.

'The problem with being invisible is you can't ask anybody the way.' Joe was moaning too.

'We can't carry this thing round for long,' he said, putting the sand box lid down on the ground. 'And I'm not leaving it anywhere while we look, so don't suggest it.'

That wasn't fair, she hadn't thought about suggesting anything. That was the trouble. Another never-stop train was slowing down in front of them.

'Come on,' said Joe, picking up the lid. 'Jump on. We've got to do something.'

The driverless train accelerated at an amazing rate, whizzing them past an enormous fair packed with amusements. Both of them wished they were free to go and have some fun but neither of them said anything. They just looked at all the children and grown-ups enjoying themselves. The never-stopping train began to slow down as it reached the long platform at Exhibition Station. Liana jumped off successfully but Joe, hampered by the weight of the lid and someone in his way, knocked his elbow as he jumped off. Liana took the lid and Joe sat down on a bench rubbing his elbow and muttering words he had probably picked up at football matches. Joe was looking at his elbow; it was red and puffy. Liana sat beside him. She knew what her father would say about the health and safety risk of a never-stopping, guard-less, driver-less train. It annoyed her to look at poor Joe and accept that her father might be right. She was thirsty and her tummy was rumbling as well.

'Hello, I'm Kaleem. I saw what happened. Can I help you?'

Liana jumped; she had been miles away in her thoughts. Only Joe had spoken to her since they left Barrow. She looked at the boy as he bent down to examine Joe's arm. He was older than they were, tall and thin. His skin was about the same colour as her friend at school in London, whose parents came from Pakistan. He spoke in a similar way too. He had thick black hair but his eyes were the colour of milk chocolate. If he could see them, then it must be for a purpose and right now they needed help. She decided to trust him so she told him about the need to find Coppernob, and how they had been travelling all day.

'You will be needing a cold water bandage on that elbow,' Kaleem told Joe.

'If you come with me I will help you.'

Joe didn't argue and even agreed to Kaleem carrying Coppernob's lid.

India's Pavilion was spectacular. There were temples with domes and towering minarets. Kaleem saw Liana looking up and told her,

'They are 110 feet high.'

She had looked at imperial measures at school and guessed that they would be about thirty metres. They were huge whichever way you measured them. There were highly decorated tiles and intricate carvings in wood and metal. There were carpets and curtains and cushions in rich reds, greens and gold. It reminded Liana of the pictures in her 'Arabian Nights' book. Kaleem took them behind a big patterned curtain where usually only the workers were allowed to go. Joe was bandaged up and Kaleem gave them both a drink of lassi, which tasted like a fruit yoghurt milk shake. It tasted strange but Liana felt much better just for that.

'I could give you some food here,' Kaleem told them. 'But you would not like it. British people are not liking our food because it is too spicy.'

Both children loved Indian food, and to Kaleem's amazement ate everything he offered them with obvious enjoyment. Liana tried to explain that they came from a time in the future when Indian food was very popular with British people. Kaleem didn't seem to be surprised by any of this.

'Time is a good healer,' Kaleem said to Joe. 'When you return to your time your elbow might be better.'

It was feeling better already. Joe was not one to hang about; there was so much to do. He picked up Coppernob's sand box lid with his good arm.

'Come on you two. We must find Coppernob. I want extra time to go on that big dipper we passed on the train, and I must see the Stadium. We might not get to play injury time here.'

'My guess is that your Coppernob engine is in the Palace of Engineering, the biggest hall in the Exhibition, covering the whole of thirteen acres.'

Liana thought Kaleem talked as if he had eaten a maths book, but he also knew a lot about the Exhibition. He took them straight to the Palace of Engineering along the side of a long lake with islands and arched bridges. Although they remembered that Coppernob and the Furness Railway had become part of the much bigger London Midland and Scottish Railway, it still took some time to find the display. They searched up and down the aisles, but when they found the display Coppernob was not there. Liana felt her palms getting hot and sticky. What if Coppernob had been sent somewhere else entirely? Kaleem went to find out. Coppernob was in a separate display called the 'Railway Centenary Historic Exhibit', and this was at the opposite end of the huge building. They were taking turns to carry the heavy lid. Kaleem took it off Liana for the last lap of its journey. It was then that the disaster happened.

'Stop thief, stop thief,' a man was shouting, as he ran along the wide walkway between the engines. All three children looked around for the thief before they realised that the shouting man was pointing at Kaleem. Instinctively they ran behind a coal wagon and out of his sight. Joe and Liana, not knowing whether they could be seen or not, stared at Kaleem holding the sand box lid. Someone, perhaps the police, thought he had stolen it.

'This way,' Joe said. He was not taking any chances. The other two followed as he dodged and swerved in and out of the spaces between the trucks, carriages and engines. He headed towards the wall where a long narrow corridor of space led down to the end of the building. Here, despite carrying the heavy lid, Kaleem's long legs took him out in front. They had almost reached the end before being spotted through a gap by a different man.

'Over there,' he yelled threateningly.

The children heard the sound of running feet coming from different directions. They were trapped; they needed a hiding place. They crept along as if they really were burglars, edging their way past a new, green engine, with a shining brass nameplate 'Caerphilly Castle'. At the front of the engine the big round smokebox door was open.

'Let's climb inside here,' Liana whispered.

11 - Time's a Thief

It was quite a distance from the floor but the buffers, bars and coupling hook, together with their fear, made it an easy climb. They all squeezed in under a cross bar pulling the door behind them.

The children, crouching in the small space stayed still and silent, each one of them hearing their own heart beating as they strained to hear the footsteps. One of the pursuers was not so quiet. A steel cap on his shoes echoed through the lofty hall with each step he took. The children listened to this tapping noise getting closer and closer. He stopped just by them. The suspense was so painful, Liana felt she wanted to jump out and get it over with, rather than suffer the dread of what might happen. She didn't move, though, and waited motionless with the others. The man must have believed that someone was still there as he hung about until he was called away. At last the listening children heard his metallic steps grow fainter and disappear. Joe sighed with relief even though they were still trapped in such a cramped place.

As they quickly and quietly climbed down from the engine, Kaleem explained about the railway carriage in the siding and his suspicions about the hoard of metal objects. He told them about his evidence and showed them his little book of dates, times and sketches. He admitted that, when he first saw Liana and Joe at Exhibition Station, he had considered whether they might be involved.

'I quickly changed my mind,' he said, 'when I realised that you were returning rather than stealing and how much you are loving Coppernob.'

'There she is,' Liana almost shouted, she was so pleased to see her. 'Look, Kaleem, that's our engine.' Liana had the lid but she gave it to Joe.

'You put it back, Joe,' Liana said, and she watched with Kaleem as Joe clipped the sand box lid over the rim and hooked on the safety chain.

'I have kept my promise to Grandad Ted and you're back in one piece again, Coppernob,' Joe said. 'And I hope you appreciate the trouble we have gone to for this.'

Kaleem laughed, but not for long; he felt a cold hand grip his collar.

'Got you. We've been watching you. You're coming with me, my lad.'

Kaleem managed to slip his little notebook to Liana before he was dragged away. Liana lifted the sand box lid and surreptitiously dropped the book inside, before running after Joe, who was diving beneath an old wagon. From there they watched and waited, hoping that they were either invisible or hidden from view. Three men were marching Kaleem out of the door at the end of the building. It didn't look as if anyone was bothering to look for them. They could have climbed up on Coppernob, pulled the reversing lever and escaped from all this. But neither Joe nor Liana would have considered leaving Kaleem, if there was any chance that they could help him.

When they were as certain as they could be that no one else was waiting for them, they scrambled out. Liana took the notebook out of the sand box, brushed off the sand and put it in her pocket.

'We had better try to find Kaleem's dad and let him know that Kaleem is not the thief and the wrong person has been caught,' she said.

All the way to the Indian Pavilion, Liana kept hoping that they would not be invisible to Kaleem's father. They found his office and knocked on the door. Kaleem's father smiled at them as he put his glasses down on the desk.

'What can I be doing for you?' he asked.

Liana showed him Kaleem's notebook. Joe explained that Kaleem had been taken away, suspected of being a thief, when all along he had been the detective. Within minutes a phone call had been made to the Exhibition office, but as the people there were unaware of any problem, another call was made to the police station. The three of them waited in silence whilst the officer on the other end of the line went off to find out what had happened.

'I'm sorry Sir, although there have been a number of items reported missing; we have not had any reports of a burglary at the Exhibition today. As far as we know, none of our men have been involved with any trouble in the Palace of Engineering.'

'In that case,' said Kaleem's father, 'I wish to report the kidnapping of my son.'

By the time the ringing bell of the police car could be heard, Joe and Liana were off to look for Kaleem themselves. They walked down to the lake and sat on a bench whilst they searched through the notebook for any clues. The drawings were so clear that both children could easily recognise the face of one of Kaleem's captors. At the end of the notebook was a map showing the position of the railway siding, Kaleem's den and the old railway carriage. They set off immediately, and had soon left the noise of the crowds behind as they stepped over railway lines and made their way into the deserted sidings. They sneaked into Kaleem's den just in time to see the three men walking away. As soon as the men had disappeared out of sight, they ran over to the old carriage, climbed up and looked inside. There was Kaleem, tied up with a gag round his mouth, lying in the piles of stolen metal.

It took little time to remove a plank of wood wedging the carriage door shut and even less time to untie Kaleem who had a nasty bulge swelling up on his forehead. 'I think you need a cold water bandage on that head,' Joe told Kaleem, who laughed despite the pins and needles in his fingers. He rubbed his hands together until the life flowed back through his unbound wrists. There was no time to waste; they raced back to the Indian Pavilion where the police were just beginning their search. Kaleem was praised for his meticulous collection of evidence. From his sketches, the three thieves were easily recognisable to the police as known criminals. Kaleem had even overheard the name of the scrap metal merchant they intended to use to pass on the stolen metal.

'You've pretty well sewn up the case for us, young man,' the chief police officer said, shaking Kaleem's hand.

At last they were free to enjoy themselves. After checking the closing time at the Palace of Engineering, they still had enough time to have some fun.

'Do you like Sir Kreemy Knut toffee?' Kaleem asked.

'Oh yeah,' Joe replied, his eyes lighting up, even though he had never heard of Sir Kreemy Knut. They went straight to an exotic kiosk decorated with palm trees and parrots. They ate their toffee assortments as they rode on a small electric bus to see the Stadium. It was really exciting for Joe to actually see the old twin towers of Wembley Stadium brilliantly white and new. He thought about the excitement in store for millions of people inside that building.

'The atmosphere is here already,' Joe said, with admiration in his voice, 'even if the title, 'The Venue of Legends' has still to be earned.'

The Canadian Pavilion was conveniently en route to the Amusement Park.

'I think I might have Canadian relations,' Liana told Kaleem.

They wandered through realistic illustrations of Canadian life with forests, snow and even wild bears. They rode through mountains on a miniature railway and Liana noticed white, pointed picket fencing everywhere, just like the fence in the photograph she had found. As they neared the Amusement Park the skyline was dominated by the sweeping curves of The Racer.

'I love this big dipper,' Kaleem told them, as he jumped aboard with Joe close behind.

'On yer get, me darlin's,' the fairground man shouted, packing the little wooden train with excited customers. Liana was taken on by the push of the crowd and the train was off before she had chance to change her mind. It clicked its way up on a moving rack to the top of the ride when gravity sent them all speeding down and over the next hump, ready for the journey up to the top of the next rise. By the time they had gone round the circuit several times, they could only stagger, laughing at their wobbly legs, to the Whirl of the World ride. The three of them sat together in an open circular car. Revolving discs in the floor sent the small cars spinning in different directions. They all had a go at steering and braking using a lever in the centre, but it didn't stop them careering off in any direction and bashing into other cars just as out of control.

The fairground lights were blazing in the gathering dusk. Little globe lights came on all over the Exhibition and Kaleem reminded them that it was time to return to Coppernob.

'The sun never sets on the British Empire,' he said, 'but it is going down now on the British Empire Exhibition.'

Liana and Joe didn't want to leave the funfair. They were sad to say goodbye to Kaleem, but Coppernob's now familiar footplate was waiting and it was time to go. As they pulled the reverser, Kaleem watched his two friends grow faint like shadows and fade from sight.

Chapter 12

A Time Bomb

THANKFULLY, only the last hour had passed in the Railway Museum whilst Joe and Liana were spending time in Barrow and in Wembley, but all other time seemed to be flying. Joe's mum had invited Liana to tea on the evening of the Christmas Show 'Bethlehem Beat'. Joe remembered his lines. The audience laughed in the right places and clapped so much at the end they had to repeat the finale. When her dad came to collect her, Liana overheard him talking to Joe's mum.

'It is certainly going to be a difficult meeting,' he said, in a lowered voice. Liana strained to hear the rest of the conversation but they were talking so quietly she missed it. There was no doubt, though, that they were talking about Coppernob.

It seemed a long time to Liana since that cold wet day when she had taken the afternoon off school to investigate The Red House basement. She was pleased because she had found helpful information about her mother, and it seemed as though she had got away with not returning to school. A few days later, however, Miss Wells asked her to stay behind after the other children had left. She sounded more concerned than cross.

'I was worried about you when you didn't return after lunch. Were you not feeling well?'

'I was fine but I had to find out something.'

'Can I help you find it?'

'No, I just wanted to know more about my mum and I had found some of her things.' Liana suddenly wanted to cry. An unbearable sorrow pushed against her throat. She had learnt not to cry, but no matter how many times she felt like this it didn't seem to get any easier. She wanted to talk to her dad. She needed the strength of a dam to hold back the tears. Time was not always a healer like Kaleem said.

'It's all right to be sad, Liana, and it would be good to know more about your mother.'

Liana nodded, words could not get past the tight lump of sadness. Miss Wells talked instead about how she missed her own grandma, especially at Christmas.

'I have the last Christmas card she sent to me. I put it out every year because I know she would send one if she could and it makes me happy to remember her. I talk to my gran in my head when I have problems and I can imagine what she would say to me, so I get an answer too. I have to get out of my flat at Christmas, of all times, so I imagine asking my gran what to do. I can hear her saying I should talk to someone. "A problem shared is a problem halved, my dear," she used to say. My gran was full of sayings like that. There, now I've told you I feel better. Maybe there is someone you could talk to who could help you?'

Liana didn't answer as the two people she most wanted to talk to, her dad and Emily, either wouldn't or couldn't talk to her. Liana had the best school report she had ever had. It was the only one that didn't say she daydreamed and could be distant. Miss Wells had written that she tried hard and was sensitive to the needs of others. That sounded like Emily, which pleased Liana. She was grateful too that she hadn't put anything about being lonely or a loner. Even more importantly Liana had full attendance, so she didn't have to explain to her father why she had been away from school on that afternoon. Miss Wells had been a brilliant teacher. Everyone was miserable when they knew that she had to go back to University after Christmas. Liana knew that she would miss her even more than the other children.

During the Christmas holidays Liana intended putting all her energy into preparing for the Coppernob meeting. On the last day of term, school finished earlier than usual. After all the 'goodbyes', Liana hurried through York to the Museum. Her mind was racing so much she hardly noticed the tourists. The 'LET COPPERNOB GO HOME' poster she was making for the meeting was beginning to take shape. She was pleased with the lettering but needed another pot of red poster paint to finish it. After calling in at Thomas the Bakers and buying four separate ginger people, so she could choose their faces, she went into Smith's in Coney Street and quickly bought the things she needed. Today she intended to finish her information gathering about Coppernob during World War 2. Before going to the Search Engine library, Liana visited Coppernob. The Museum notice, under a picture of Coppernob in her glass pagoda case in Barrow, said that she had been badly damaged by shrapnel in 1941. Liana ran her hand over Coppernob's holes and dents. She winced at the thought of her being pounded with exploding metal. At least Grandad Ted never knew that Coppernob was bombed. What had Grandad Ted said?

'She was my life, that engine,' Liana was beginning to understand how he felt.

Liana had visited the Search Engine up on the Gallery a number of times already and had collected, in a small notebook, the information she thought would provide good evidence to be used at the Coppernob meeting. The explainer at the entrance winked at Liana as he wrote what she was looking for in his book.

'It's Miss Coppernob, isn't it?' he asked with a big smile.

Liana picked a big book about stations off the shelf to look at whilst she waited for her request to be found in the archives. Some photographs of

country stations looked similar to those on the Furness Railway but there were none she recognised.

'I've photocopied an old list I've found for you about Barrow-in-Furness being bombed'.

Liana was startled by a young lady waving a piece of paper. She had not expected to get anything so quickly, but she had hoped for a book or pamphlet with pictures.

'I am really sorry it is difficult to read but it is as good as the original'. She handed Liana a badly typed, fuzzy photocopy, offered to look again then disappeared back into the archives. Liana felt really thirsty so she walked back down the stairs and round to the Dining Car café. She bought herself an orange juice and sipped it slowly through a straw. She wondered about doing her poster, but she couldn't get a 'LET COPPERNOB GO HOME' poster out of her bag here.

The feint, photocopied list was still in her hand. Liana turned her attention to it and tried to decipher what it could possibly mean. The headings were unclear and the first line did not seem to make much sense. In the first column was the date - that was easy and probably meant late night on the 4th and early morning on the 5th May. As she read down the list, however, she could see that in the second column were places. The third column seemed to be in a kind of code:

1941

4/5 MAY	HAYES TIMBER YARD	2 IB's

4/5 MAY	THE PUBLIC PARK,	1 HE
	DIRECT HIT 2 SUTTON ROAD,	1 LM
	CORNER SHOP- PENNINGTON STREET,	1 IB UE
	CENTRAL STATION ENTRANCE,	1 HE
	NUMBER 1 PLATFORM.	1 HE

Liana looked more carefully at the third heading and could just make out 'TYPE OF BOMB'. Some had UE after them. What did that mean? This must have been the night when Coppernob was damaged. Liana froze as her eye caught one address she recognised:

1941

4/5 MAY	DIRECT HIT No 26 CHADWICK STREET	1 HE UE

This was Grandad Ted's house in 1912 and Liana felt sure that when he died in 1925 Emily, George and baby Anna would have stayed living there. Did they still live there in May 1941? Could it be possible that they were killed by a German bomb? Emily, born in 1900, would be 41 years old and George a little older. Baby Anna would be about sixteen. Liana felt sick at the thought. Were they all killed whilst sleeping in their beds? Was it possible to do anything about this? Liana found an explainer and asked her if she could decipher the wartime code.

'I can have a good guess,' she said, 'I'm sure that LM stands for Land Mine and HE for High Explosive.' IB took her a little longer but she suddenly thought of Incendiary Bomb and explained about them setting things on fire. UE didn't mean anything to her. She offered to find out, but Liana was beginning to feel panic. Emily was her closest friend, she would have to at least try to do something to warn her. Liana thought of Grandad Ted's words:

'There is a time for every purpose.'

If ever that was true it was true now. She had to go back to Barrow-in-Furness, but how could she pick the time and place? She would go right now, alone.

She did not expect to find Joe in the Museum, but as soon as Liana reached the little yellow signal box she could see his dirty grey trainers through the window.

'Start again, who gets bombed?' Joe couldn't understand what Liana was saying. She was talking too quickly.

'Look, it says, '1941 4/5 May, Direct Hit No 26 Chadwick Street 1 HE UE,' here! HE stands for High Explosive,' Liana pointed at the photocopied sheet. Joe took hold of the sheet and read for himself.

'The station is bombed on the same night,' he said, suddenly realising why Liana was so concerned but still surprised by her determination.

'I've decided to try No 3, Detonators,' Liana said, looking at the signal levers. 'Are you coming?'

Joe only had time to nod before, with great purpose, she squeezed and pulled the lever down. As the walls began to spin and they felt themselves falling, Joe wondered about Liana. Had he misjudged her or had she changed? Liana, meanwhile, eyes tight shut, was repeating silently,

'Please, please, please let it be before 4th May 1941.'

They stopped. Liana opened her eyes but still couldn't see. Everywhere was pitch-black and deathly silent. They were in an empty signal box somewhere, but where? Liana could just make out the shape of the windows. Joe had landed near the door and found the handle as he stood up. There was no moon. Outside looked just as black at first, but as they stepped out Liana stopped.

'I recognise the feel of this place,' she shuddered as she remembered Emily's terrible father and the train that had so nearly run over her.

'This is Barrow-in-Furness South signal box. Over there is the station. If you keep looking, Joe, you should make out the shape.'

It was lit by dim, eerie blue lights. Joe peered in the right direction.

'Well, it's not bombed yet then,' he said in his usual, cheerful manner.

They made their way towards the station along the cinder track following the rails. Liana was looking for the houses behind the long brick wall but everywhere was so dark. They would have to cross over the lines to the station, then double back across the road bridge over the railway, to get behind the long brick wall to Chadwick Street. As they neared the station Joe pointed out the lamps covered with what looked like dark blue paper.

'I think this must be wartime, Liana. It's all so dark because they have to black out all the lights to stop the German bombers seeing where places are.'

'In that case listen carefully in case a train is coming, as we need to cross the lines here. Maybe the trains won't have lights either.'

'I expect,' Joe reasoned, 'the passengers sit in blackout gloom, which must be very strange. If the train windows weren't blacked out the German planes could just follow the golden snake to the next town and bomb it. Snakes you lose. The train drivers would have to hide the fire but they would need some light to see where they were going. Perhaps they would stop if they could hear a plane.'

Liana was not really listening to Joe. She was glad to have reached the platform, but she still felt the chill of fear, everywhere was so unbelievably

quiet. They crept along into the station building past a stand with a big notice, '**W·H·SMITH & SON**'. It felt a long way and long time since she was buying poster paint in the brilliantly lit Smith's in York. Liana went straight to the booking hall and looked at the clock. It was almost 9 o'clock but what was the date? She left Joe and ran back to the bookstall. There were just a few newspapers still there, clipped under a wire. She read the date, 4th May 1941.

How much time would they have before the bombs started falling? Would they have time to give a warning? They ran out of the front of the station and along the side of Coppernob in her glass case.

'Hold tight, Coppernob, you'll survive,' whispered Liana, knowing that Coppernob would never be the same again after this night. As they crossed the road bridge, one man with a dog scuttled off in the opposite direction, but otherwise they were quite alone. They kept close to the long brick wall down Chadwick Street and only crossed over opposite number 26. Liana knocked, they waited, nothing. She knocked a bit louder with George's five knocks to Bar-row-in-Fur-ness and saw a small flicker of light behind the upstairs

12 - A Time Bomb

blackout. Joe put his hand up to knock again but Liana stopped him.

'They're coming,' she said.

Quietly the door opened and even in the dark Liana knew who it was.

'Emily,' she whispered, 'it's Liana.'

Emily opened the door just wide enough and hurried them in, shutting the door behind them before giving Liana a big hug. Emily was older but not so very different really.

'This is not a good time to come here,' Emily began, 'there is a war on. Barrow-in-Furness, as a ship-building town, is a target for air raids; what with the steelworks and the railway as well, we have already suffered casualties.'

'That is why we have come,' said Joe. 'Tonight your house gets a direct hit from a German high explosive bomb. Liana found a list in the Museum.'

Emily looked stunned. Just for a second Liana thought she might not believe them, but Emily hesitated only briefly whilst she decided what to do.

'We must act quickly, I'll wake my Anna,' she said.

'And George too,' added Liana, but Emily was already upstairs.

'No, George is not here,' she shouted down, 'he travels all over the country now. The war has created so many problems for the railways.'

Emily wasted no time and soon returned with Anna. They were both wearing coats and carrying small tin cases. Anna at sixteen would not be recognisable from the tiny baby they had held before. Now she had the same dark curly hair as her father George and clear blue eyes like Ted, her great-grandad. Anna smiled.

'My mother has talked about you both and how I was named Liana after you, although I am usually just called Anna. I don't remember you. I was too young.'

'Liana, tell me where else was hit?' Emily asked calmly, but urgently. Liana told her about the station and other places she remembered from the list, which must have been left behind in the little yellow signal box. Emily looked purposefully at the three of them.

'You go to the station, warn them. Tell them we must sound the air-raid siren. I'll spread the word here and get my neighbours into the shelters. Go, God be with you.'

She squeezed Liana's hand, kissed Anna on the cheek and was gone, knocking on the neighbour's doors and shouting through the letterboxes. Anna gave Joe her torch, which had a hood over the top to stop the light shining up.

'See you there,' she said, and was gone so quickly, by the time Joe switched on the slit of light from the torch, they only caught the last glimpse of Anna disappearing down Chadwick Street. Liana and Joe followed as fast as they could back along the street and across the silent road bridge to the empty station. They stood outside the stationmaster's office and could just hear Anna's firm but quietly anxious voice through the door. Liana tried to listen over the sound of her own heart thumping.

'Please believe her, please,' murmured Liana.

They waited in the ghostly quiet of the station, straining to hear until a sudden, piercingly loud sound made them both leap away from the door. The shrill of the siren seemed to fill every breath of air, wailing a warning to the whole of Barrow-in-Furness.

'You've done what you came to do, Liana, you have warned everyone and they know what to do. We can go now,' said Joe, brushing his fingers through his hair. 'Let's get on Coppernob.'

Liana hesitated, something wasn't right and she didn't want to leave without saying goodbye. They walked out of the station and round to Coppernob's glass pagoda, which loomed above them in the darkness. They could just make out the black shape of the chimney against the glass but it was difficult to see Coppernob clearly.

Joe tried the door. It was locked.

Chapter 13

Killing Time

ANNA Matthews came out of Barrow Central Station urgently beckoning Joe and Liana to follow her. By the time they caught up they were out of the station forecourt and in a street of small, terraced houses. Anna seemed to know everyone by name and was calling to see if they needed help getting into the shelters.

'Help Mrs Watson,' Liana was told, as she stumbled into a darkened house. Mrs Watson wouldn't budge without her insurance policies and ration book, but fortunately they were quickly found in a drawer. Clutching her tin box and the little leather document case, Mrs Watson hurried as best she could, with Liana's help, down the street to a shared shelter at the end. Joe was using the hooded torch to help people down the dark stairs leading into the shelter, which hummed with urgent chatter but looked quite comfortable inside. As soon as Anna was satisfied that there were enough people organising and helping those who needed it, she turned to Liana and Joe.

'I'm goin' to try to get back to Mum, she'll need help and there should be enough time.'

As they ran back towards the station they could hear the dull, growling rumble of a plane.

'It's the Luftwaffe,' Anna said, stopping still and looking scared for the first time. A tremendous explosion shook the ground so violently, it felt more like a volcano coming up from underneath than a bomb dropped down from above.

'Quick, I know where we can go,' Anna shouted, as she carried on running towards the station.

'Bad idea,' grumbled Joe, but not knowing what else to do they followed her into the wide station forecourt. Anna led them to a small shed directly opposite Coppernob. It was mostly underground with a corrugated iron roof. The shed was being used as a sand bag store so they could make themselves fairly comfortable. They were just about to close the door when the sky was lit up by a powerful beam of light. As it searched for German planes they could see the black silhouettes of Barrow's towers, cranes and chimneys. Then they saw Coppernob. She looked proud and brave as a second huge explosion ripped through the air. They backed into the makeshift shelter pulling the door as tightly as it would fit. The planes moved over to target the shipyards, the fires now blazing, lighting their way. Liana thought the heavy drone of the engines was as threatening as the bombs themselves. It was like being in a thunderstorm waiting for the lightning to strike, only so much worse.

Anna had water in an old lemonade bottle and a few biscuits in her bag. Despite everything, they all felt like eating. The biscuits were soft and tasteless. Joe looked hopefully at Anna's tin case.

'I'm sorry,' she said, 'all that's in here is my gas mask.'

Joe tried it on but didn't like the smell. He shook his head.

'And I thought they were all taking their packed lunches into the shelter.'

Liana reached into her pocket and from a scrunched up paper bag she pulled out her four ginger people. Joe enjoyed eating his because he was hungry but Anna thought hers, especially the Smartie face, tasted wonderful. She told them that they had rations, which meant each person could only have a little sugar and not many sweets. Anna explained how they couldn't get food that came from abroad. She also told them that many other things were not so good because of the war. Liana gave Anna another ginger person and wrapped the fourth one in the paper bag and put it back in her pocket for Emily.

The planes had passed over for the time being, although they all believed that the calm would not last long. There was so much to say. Anna asked them so many questions, and like Kaleem she had no trouble understanding that they had travelled backwards in time. She asked Joe what young people did to have fun in the twenty-first century. She listened, fascinated, trying to imagine what he meant by the Internet and computer games. Anna really liked the idea of big shopping centres with no queues, and televisions with coloured pictures like a cinema in your own home. Joe told her about supporting Manchester United and they all laughed when she said that didn't sound very different!

Anna listened carefully whilst Liana described the problem with Coppernob. Liana told her how she was supporting the people of Barrow in trying to get the old engine out of the Museum in York and back into the Barrow-in-Furness shopping centre.

'I feel sure this is what Ted, your great-grandad, would have wanted,' Liana explained.

Anna did not look so sure, but Liana didn't notice as the planes could be heard returning. She moved to sit by the slightly open door and watched as the furious fireworks began to boom and crackle, lighting up the sky once again, before a gloomy black stillness settled back around them. Liana's stomach felt tight; she knew what she was looking for. In the inky darkness the searchlight caught the plane just as the bomb was dropping. Liana opened the door to try and see where it landed. She knew it would hit Emily's house. There was no explosion, just a sickening thud. Anna and Joe stood with her at the door.

'I know now what UE means,' Liana said, feeling a strange relief. 'UN-EXPLODED.'

Not so the next bomb, a direct hit on target. The station exploded into flying fragments. Even before they came down to earth another bomb hit the tracks and another the platform. As if in slow motion Coppernob's tall case shattered.

Lit by a brilliant flash of light, shards of tinkling, silver glass fell like an avalanche. They shut the shed door and dived into the sand bags as pieces of wood, metal and glass hit the tin roof and clouds of dust filled the air. They waited, listening hard until the last menacing hum of the aircraft had gone. They struggled out of the shelter coughing and choking. The air was so thick with dirt and smoke, they could scarcely breathe. The station had become a heap of toppling masonry and twisted metal. Broken bricks and rubble lay scattered all around. But there through the grey mist, boldly resistant, standing alone was Coppernob, her tall chimney pointing defiantly up into the sky.

It was difficult to get over the mangled mess of broken glass and splintered wood. Even Coppernob's concrete base had crumbled and a huge piece of metal was wedged in Coppernob's side. Joe tried to yank it out but it wouldn't come, and he was having difficulty with a sharp splinter of glass sticking out of his trainer. Looking at Coppernob, her copper firebox covered with dirt and debris, Liana felt even more sure that after all this, the engine belonged in Barrow. She would go to the meeting, fight her father and win.

Anna, although relieved to see Coppernob still in one piece, was already picking her way through the rubble back to her mother and her home. A siren was sounding the 'all clear'. Even Liana and Joe could guess its meaning and feel the relief, but not for long. When they arrived at 26 Chadwick Street Emily was already outside the house, with her neighbours, looking at the huge metal bomb wedged in the doorway. The front wall of the house had gone leaving it open like a doll's house. Amazingly, most things were still standing as they had been, although everything was covered in dust and soot from the chimney. Emily's beautiful teapot collection was lying smashed on what must still have been the carpet, underneath the debris.

Emily and Anna hugged each other, so relieved to be alive and unharmed. Anna's arrival brought Emily round from her dazed shock. With quiet courage, Emily started to move the mesmerized people down the street away from the danger.

'Move away now, help each other,' Emily told them. 'Go to the church hall. You will be cared for there until temporary accommodation can be found.'

Liana and Joe stood across the road by the long brick wall and watched as the people started to move away. One older lady was not going though.

'My cat Rumpelstiltskin is still in there somewhere,' Emily's next door neighbour was convinced. 'He is all I've got, I must look for him.' She shouted, 'Rumpels, Rumpels.' in a thin, distressed voice but there was no cat.

'Your cat has nine lives, Alice,' Emily said putting her arm around her and leading her to Anna. 'You only have one. Rumpels will be safe, just you wait and see.' Anna helped Alice up to the church hall. By the time an army lorry was making its way down the littered street, Emily was moving the last of the people away.

'Thank you, love,' said a soldier, looking more worried than he sounded as he saw the huge silver bomb with its nose buried straight down into the place that had been Emily's front door.

'Best be movin' along yourself now.'

Emily hesitated, but after one last look at her already shattered home and the menacing unexploded bomb, she turned and hurried away to catch up with the others.

Liana and Joe set off back towards the station and Coppernob in silence.

'I'm still not ready to go,' Liana said, stopping and looking straight at Joe. 'I can't go without saying goodbye. It just doesn't feel right.'

'OK,' Joe agreed. 'How do we get to the church hall?'

Liana remembered seeing the church hall when they had pushed Anna in her pram up the hill to the cemetery. It was opposite Emily's school.

'I know a short cut from here,' she told Joe.

Liana was hurrying up the same streets she had hurried along to school with Emily on her first visit to Barrow. Now, a cloud of dust hung in the air like a fog, making their eyes smart. Joe held his nose. There was a strong smell like a strange mixture of burning paper and damp cellars. The houses that had once huddled together now seemed pulled apart. Windows had been blown out and fragments of glass and brick lay scattered in the dust. The roofs and fronts of two houses had been completely removed. You could see the ruined beds, tables and chairs just as if a child had smashed their toys.

The church hall buzzed with the organisation of tea and blankets being given and taken, and accommodation being offered and accepted. Some people talked readily whilst others stared blankly. The children could feel the positive atmosphere as friends and neighbours supported and comforted each other. Emily stood up at the front; the room quietened as she spoke.

'Those of us in need of help, would like to thank all of you who are offering to share your homes and your rations with us. We need to stick together and be kind to one another. This bombing is designed not just to destroy our steel works, shipyard and railway but also to destroy our spirit and morale, and in that way break down our war production. To defeat our enemies we must stiffen our determination, making sure that they will never win.'

Joe and Liana, and Anna too, marvelled at the power and conviction in gentle Emily's voice. A cheer rang through the hall as the three of them slipped outside.

'My poor mother was so concerned to wake the neighbours that she didn't take her little box of important documents with her.' Anna told them. 'She keeps the box under the stairs, so if that bomb in our doorway goes off we will lose so many important papers. She keeps our birth certificates and insurance policies in the box and other things too.'

'You should get it back,' Joe said reassuringly. 'It did show the bomb remained unexploded on our Museum list.'

Anna hugged them both. 'I hope you are right. Do come back when things are better next time,' she pleaded.

'We will,' Liana answered. 'Please say goodbye to Emily for me and give her this.' She handed Anna the crumpled bag with the remaining ginger person inside.

For the second time Liana and Joe set off back to the station and Coppernob. As they neared Chadwick Street they could see that barriers had been erected to stop anyone entering the danger zone. Joe kept on walking.

'Where are you going?' Liana asked, but she already knew the answer.

'To get the box of papers for Emily,' Joe replied, skirting round the barrier and heading straight for number 26. The sky was lightening into morning, but the soldier on duty at the end of the street didn't see them. Perhaps he couldn't see them or maybe he was too interested in eating his doorstep size sandwich and drinking tea from his tin mug.

They walked through the gap where the front window had once been and picked their way round the scattered broken pieces of their friend's home. It was then they heard the ticking. Both of them stopped still as statues and looked at the bomb. The ticking continued but was joined by a whirring noise and the clear chiming of a clock striking four. Joe brushed his fingers through his hair before carefully opening the door of the cupboard under the stairs. He took out the dusty but unharmed box whilst Liana was searching on the floor beneath the fireplace. First she found the clock and put it back on the mantle piece but then she found what she was looking for. The glass was broken but she was able to blow the soot and dust away. It was the picture of Grandad Ted on Coppernob. It was just as they were leaving they heard the 'meow'. There, sitting right beside the bomb was a big, baggy, marmalade cat.

'Rumpels,' Liana called but the cat just stared at her. She gave Joe the picture to hold, crossed over to the bomb and picked up the cat. Rumpels seemed to stretch out as he was lifted. Liana had to balance him on her knee whilst she got a better grasp. At last they left the house and made their way back to the church hall.

They soon found Emily and Joe gave her the box. For the first time she looked tearful, but she smiled and hugged them both.

'I think of you often,' Liana told her.

'And I think of you too,' Emily replied. 'Ours is a strange but special friendship. It is my wish that you find what you are searching for, Liana.'

Anna took the precious picture of her great-grandfather and Coppernob and promised to tell her dad, George, that they were sorry they had missed him. She hugged them just like her mother. Rumpels had jumped out of Liana's arms as soon as he saw Alice. It would be difficult to say who looked the most content, the old lady or the cat. For the third and last time Liana and Joe set off back to the station.

'Wait, wait,' it was Anna waving an envelope in her hand.

'Mum said you wanted this letter about Coppernob, written by my great-grandfather Ted. She found it soon after your last visit and has kept it safe for you for all this time. It was in the box you rescued for us.'

Liana, with all her concern about the bomb, had forgotten how much she had wanted this letter. She put it carefully in her pocket. By the time they reached Coppernob Joe was limping badly. Liana helped him over the rubble and on to the footplate. She carefully wiped some of the dirt from the dented firebox until she could see the copper still golden underneath.

'Hold on Joe,' she said, as she squeezed and pulled the reverser.

Coppernob seemed to lurch; they both held on tightly as they hurtled back through time to the Railway Museum.

94

13 - Killing Time

Time for Coppernob

The Museum was quiet except for Joe who was complaining miserably about the hole in his trainer. He had taken it off and could stick his finger right through the sole.

'You had better get your foot seen to.' Liana was looking at his sock stuck with blood and dirt to his foot, but Joe had not yet noticed that.

'The rain will get in now and a new pair will never be as comfortable,' he moaned. 'And Peter will go on about the stupid excuse I wrote for him for PE.'

'We did a good job, Joe. Our friends in Barrow were not hurt and we are back safely. And new trainers will soon go grey.'

It was Liana's turn to make Joe smile. They climbed carefully down off Coppernob and Liana inspected the damage done by the metal shaft, whilst Joe examined his foot.

'Looks like they made a hole in my foot as well as my shoe,' Joe muttered. 'I know how you feel, Coppernob.'

He started to hobble back to his mum's office, carrying his trainer, whilst Liana went back to the little yellow signal box to collect her things. Instead of going straight to meet her father she walked back to Coppernob and ran her hand over the biggest hole in the boiler.

'Well done Coppernob,' she said. 'No way could the Luftwaffe knock our brave little engine off her pedestal.'

Chapter 14

Time to Remember

IT was very late by the time Liana put Grandad Ted's letter back in its
envelope, climbed out of bed and hid it away safely. She kept it with her
other treasures, in the shoebox at the back of her wardrobe. The letter
had raised urgent questions in her mind; she had read it and re-read it many
times. Liana was still only half asleep when the birds started to twitter. She
was too exhausted either to sleep peacefully or to think clearly. She got up late
the next day, thankful for the Christmas holidays. For once Liana was glad to
be alone in The Red House. Travelling around the country, changing times
and seasons was tiring, even without the problem solving she seemed to be
constantly faced with. Joe had forgotten his reticence and phoned Liana to
find out what was in Grandad Ted's letter. He listened intently whilst she read
it to him. When she had finished, Liana heard him release his breath.

'That throws quite a different light upon the problem,' he said.

Christmas helped to take Liana's mind off the prospect of the Coppernob
meeting to some extent, but still the conflicts and contradictions pressed upon
her. Just as Joe had been desperate to keep his promise to Grandad Ted
and return Coppernob's sand box lid, Liana felt that with the letter came a
deep responsibility. Coppernob was never mentioned but Mark Emerson
seemed to be making an effort to talk to his daughter. They shopped together,
decorated the tree and hung dark green holly with bright berries on the red
front door. Uncle Adrian came to stay and the atmosphere in The Red House
became more relaxed and comfortable. However, Coppernob was not the
only problem Liana badly needed to settle. She would wait for the right time,
but she had every intention of finding out from her father the truth about her
mother. She would handle it better this time though.

Liana decided to spend her Christmas money on a camera of her own. She
wanted to take a photograph of Coppernob. Uncle Adrian helped her to
choose a camera. Liana enjoyed his company when her father had gone back
to work. He explained to Liana why he used a tripod and the different lenses
he kept in a little bag. Her camera was nothing like his but hers was exactly
what she wanted, small with a built-in flash and a soft leather case. They
spent a day in York taking photographs of the Minster and the engines in the
Museum. Liana's best photograph of Coppernob, they all had to agree, was
better than the same picture taken by Uncle Adrian with all his photography
equipment. One afternoon they went down to the basement to look for the old

camera Liana had noticed down there. Liana found the camera quickly and whilst Uncle Adrian was looking at it, she collected the post cards he had sent to her father and her mother.

'You knew my mother, didn't you?' Liana asked, handing him the postcards knowingly.

'Yes, I liked your mother very much. She was always lots of fun to be with.'

'I remember her too and I need to know more about her. Will you tell me?'

'Your father could tell you a lot more than me.'

'But he won't, that's the trouble.' Liana could feel the familiar tension gathering in her throat.

'I will talk to Mark,' Uncle Adrian said, to the air rather than Liana, but he turned his attention back to her.

'Your father is a loner like me, Liana. He doesn't find it easy to talk about the things that mean the most to him. He loves you more than anything in the world. Perhaps he is afraid of losing your love now you are growing up.'

Uncle Adrian handed the postcards back to Liana, ending the discussion. Like her father and probably all grown-ups, he was skilful at changing the conversation, but Liana had succeeded in the first part of her plan.

'Come on, let's have a look at this camera and make a cup of tea. It's getting cold down here. Mark should let this basement flat. It hardly needs any work doing on it and it would be better to have other people in the house. I'm sure he could let it easily.'

Liana could hardly believe it. Why hadn't she thought of this herself? Was she too late or might her teacher, Miss Wells, want The Red House basement as her flat?

It was the last night of Uncle Adrian's stay. This time he invited Liana and her father to go out with him for an Indian meal. He always took Mark out at the end of his visits, but in the past Liana had stayed at home with a sitter. She was very pleased to go with them this time. They ordered different dishes to share, which always seemed such a friendly way to eat. She wasn't questioned about her choice of lassi to drink, as many of the dishes she helped to choose were new to her. The lassi was not quite as good as the drink Kaleem had given her in the British Empire Exhibition, but it had a distinct yoghurt flavour she remembered well. Eventually, Uncle Adrian spoke to her father about the basement flat.

'It is a good idea, Adrian,' her father said, 'but I'd need to be quite certain that the occupants were trustworthy. I would consider a permanent tenant but not holiday lets.'

'My teacher wanted another flat,' Liana joined in. 'She might have found somewhere else by now; please can I try and find out?' Liana waited only a few moments for her answer, but the time it took for her father to finish his mouthful of food and take a sip of wine felt like forever.

'You can find out if you wish, but we would need to buy curtains and furniture before it would be ready.'

Liana didn't think that would be a problem at all.

The weather was cold and the days were short and dark, but on the Saturday of the Coppernob meeting the sky was bright and clear. Jenny had given Liana all the information she needed. The meeting would be held in the Evening Star Lecture Theatre and it would start at 2.00 pm. Grandad Ted's letter was in Liana's pocket. She kept a tight hold of it all the way to the Museum. She had to keep checking that it was still there and would not somehow disappear before the meeting. Her father had gone off to work early and she had spent the morning reading and re-reading the letter. She had phoned Joe twice to check that he would be at the meeting, but he was playing an away match and would not be home until lunchtime. Liana really wanted Joe to be there in case she needed some help.

The walk across York took ages compared with after school. Liana had forgotten that the tourist season lasted all year. The many cafés were pouring out well-fed customers whilst hungry ones tried to get in. Groups of people stood in the way eating fish and chips and other things out of paper bags. Despite the chill in the air, there probably wasn't a spare seat on a bench left anywhere. You might have thought Thomas the Bakers were having a half-price sale given the queue trailing down Church Street. Liana crossed the road and fought her way past the crowds watching the Morris dancers in St Sampson's Square. She could only see the occasional scarf flick out above the heads but the jingling bells and clattering clogs made her feel tense and nervous. She should have chosen a different route.

Despite the hassle getting there, Liana was in plenty of time. There was a queue to get into the Museum but Jenny was welcoming the visitors, giving them information and getting them in and organised quickly. As usual she smiled at everyone but she was even more pleased to see Liana. She knew Liana would be going to the meeting.

'We have to stick up for what we truly believe in,' Jenny said. 'I'm going to try to get into the meeting too, I finish in half an hour. Best of luck.'

Jenny didn't know Liana intended to speak and needed all the luck she could get just at that moment. Not wanting to go in too soon, Liana walked around the Great Hall. She had also forgotten how busy the Museum gets in the daytime, especially on a Saturday. Little children dashed about squealing with delight or stared spellbound. Older ones, impatient to see everything, moved round purposefully, intent on making all things moveable move. Coppernob had plenty of visitors and Liana could hear an explainer answering questions about her. Children always wanted to know why she had so many holes. He sounded like a teacher with such a loud clear voice. Would she be able to speak up well enough? She didn't know.

The lecture theatre was filling up and Joe had not arrived yet. Liana had found a good seat near the back by the door and had left just one place on the outside, which hopefully no one would take before Joe arrived. She checked the letter for at least the hundredth time. It was still there but she could hear her heart thumping even above the chattering people taking their seats. Would she ever have the courage to read it out? Then she remembered the girl she sat next to in school with Emily. What was her name? Ivy, Ivy Tanner. If Ivy could manage to read out loud when she found the words difficult, Liana had to try; she owed it to Grandad Ted and to Coppernob. As the doors were shutting, in came Joe with his Mum and Peter. They all sat just behind her as Mr Stubbs, a man she recognised from the Museum, stood to open the meeting.

'Good afternoon, Ladies and Gentlemen. On behalf of The National Railway Museum, I would like to welcome you all, especially those who have travelled from Barrow-in-Furness to be at this meeting today. Many of us here have strong views about the future of the Furness Railway engine Number 3, 'Old Coppernob'. This meeting has been called so that we can give our views and debate the issues. Let us all remember, that despite our differences, we have in common the preservation of Coppernob and the history of the people whose lives have been connected with her. I call upon Councillor Mrs Askew of Barrow-in-Furness to open the meeting with the Council's proposals to house Coppernob within the shopping precinct development. Councillor Askew ...'

Councillor Askew was well-prepared and delivered a convincing explanation of the proposals. On the screen behind her, she flashed up her main points and photographs of the area using the latest technology. She showed the proposed site and counteracted questions about security with artist's drawings of the positioning of security cameras and alarms. At the end of her speech, although Mrs Askew was applauded politely by everyone, it was obvious where the Barrow contingent were sitting as they clapped the loudest, muttering

'Here, here,' and other signs of agreement.

14 - Time to Remember

'I would now like to call upon Dr Emerson of The National Railway Museum, York, to give you the case for keeping Coppernob at the Museum. Dr Emerson ...'

All eyes were on Liana's father. He did not use any technology. As he spoke he leant upon the high desk as if he wanted to push it over to get closer to his audience. His confidence and conviction held their attention. He recalled the early days of the Museum in Clapham and the reasons for housing the exhibits together. He stressed the need to build and care for the collections so that more people could benefit from seeing them. He then spoke of Coppernob. He explained how, as the only surviving example of an early bar-framed construction, Coppernob played a unique part in the Museum's display of locomotives. Without Coppernob they would be unable to represent all the different stages of railway development in Great Britain. This time it was the Friends of the Railway Museum who clapped the loudest. There was no shortage of people from both sides clamouring to speak. Liana listened as good arguments were presented for both sides of the case. She took Grandad Ted's letter out of her pocket and raised her hand to speak.

Mr Stubbs was drawing the discussion to a close.

'We will take one more speaker.'

Liana stood up feeling herself shaking, but with a determination she had never felt before and her father would never have imagined she could possess.

'Excuse me,' Liana began, 'but I would like to bring to your notice a letter. It was written on, 11th March 1925 by Mr Ted Matthews. Mr Matthews was a fireman and later an engine driver with the Furness Railway. He spent most of his life working with Coppernob. In fact the Museum has a photograph of him in its collection. I would like to read the letter to you.'

There were some mumblings from the Museum supporters and Dr Emerson stared at his daughter, his face frozen but his eyes burning.

26 Chadwick Street,
Barrow-in-Furness,
11th March 1925.

To Whom This May Concern,

My interest in the engine Coppernob goes back as far as I can remember. She and I arrived in this world in the year of our Lord 1846. By the time I became her fireman she had pulled the first passenger train and had seen the great expansion of the Furness Railway. Coppernob, FR number 3, was brought from Liverpool to Barrow by sea with her sister engine number 4. Numbers 1 and 2 had arrived earlier to help in the building of the line. Number 1 was scrapped in 1866 following a severe fire and number 2 was sold in 1871. Numbers 3 and 4 gave continued service to the Furness Railway, just as I did for 50 years. Coppernob was withdrawn from service in 1899 and should have been scrapped, as was engine number 4, in 1900.

I have shared all my working life with Coppernob, as fireman and later as her driver. Nobody could love and respect her more than I do. However, all those who worked with her, saw her working, or travelled as passengers, loved her too. The people of Barrow in those days knew her to be hard working, gentle and reliable. We decided to preserve our engine so that future generations could see their history for themselves. It has been good and fitting that Coppernob has for over twenty years been displayed in a magnificent glass case, in her own home town, at the entrance to Barrow Central Station.

It is my wish, however, that one day our country will follow the example of the people of Barrow and understand the importance of preserving engines like Coppernob. Coppernob has played an important part in British history, not just the history of Barrow-in-Furness. My dream and my hope for the future is that one day a museum will be built big enough to house many engines, showing the history of the railways of Great Britain. Coppernob should have pride of place there.

With proper care Coppernob can live on forever. I, on the other hand, have lived a long time and have little time left in this world. I leave you with my wish.

Yours faithfully,
Ted Matthews

A strange stillness had fallen over the room and Liana did not hesitate to deliver the message she was now so certain was right.

'Many people don't live with their families but enjoy being with them when they visit. Coppernob must be part of the permanent display here in the Railway Museum in York, but this should not stop her from making trips back to visit the people in Barrow, her home town.'

When the last echo of Liana's voice died away there was silence, but the faces said more than enough for Liana. For the first time she realised that everyone was looking at her. Some looked annoyed even angry, whereas others were nodding, almost smiling. Her father was still staring at her but his look had changed. He was obviously shocked but was that admiration she could see? Liana sat down, putting the letter safely back in her pocket. Suddenly everyone seemed to be talking and Mr Stubbs had to bang on the desk to get quiet. Councillor Askew raised her hand to speak again.

'How do we know this letter is genuine?'

Liana, with rising panic, tried to think of convincing words. She could not tell the truth, as nobody would believe her and lies stuck in her throat. She turned to Joe who just for once looked lost for words but nevertheless slowly raised his hand. Tension was rising as an old lady at the front slowly stood up and faced the audience. All eyes were on her now and the room fell quiet once more.

'My name is Anna. Before I was married I was Anna Matthews and it is my letter. I know that it is genuine because it was given to my mother Emily, Ted Matthew's grandaughter, who was there when it was written. It was rescued when our house was damaged in the Second World War. It has been kept safe in the hope that one day my great-grandfather's wish would be fulfilled. I gave the letter to Liana Emerson when I found out how much she cared about Coppernob. It is so sad to see all this disagreement when everyone here shares Liana's concern and appreciates the need to preserve Coppernob's history. I believe that if Ted Matthews could be here today he would tell you how Coppernob travelled to Wembley, to be displayed at the British Empire Exhibition, where thousands of people benefited from seeing her. My own father George Matthews would have been able to continue the story with Coppernob visiting Carlisle Citadel in 1958 before being moved to Clapham. Surely it cannot be beyond our ability to display Coppernob for the nation in York and arrange for her to make visits home to Barrow? I leave you with my great-grandad Ted's favourite words. There is a time for every purpose.'

Mr Stubbs ended the meeting with the promise of further negotiations but no one was listening now. Joe's mum patted Liana's shoulder.

'Well done, love.'

'Yeah, you were brilliant,' added Peter, which was a surprise as Liana had hardly heard him speak before. Joe was grinning. Liana smiled at them all, but when she turned round Anna had disappeared. Her seat was empty. It seemed everyone was talking now; the people huddled in groups around the room and those moving towards the doors. Her father was talking to

Councillor Askew and a small queue of people was forming to talk to them. Where had Anna gone?

'I'm here,' she said, seeing Liana scanning the room. 'Come on, let's go and see Coppernob.'

For Anna it had been a very long time since the war. Her dark curly hair had become white as Coppernob's steam. She had many wrinkles now and she looked smaller. Although she was very old, Anna still had a twinkle in her bright blue eyes and she managed to push through the crowd without any difficulty. They sat on a bench together just inside the Great Hall.

'After the war when my mum, Emily, was alive we used to talk about you and wonder whether you would come back. I have thought about you over the years and I have been reminded of you recently with all the stories in the newspapers about Coppernob. I wondered if you would still have the letter after all this time, but of course it is not that long for you is it?'

Liana shook her head.

'It doesn't seem so long to me any more', Anna continued. 'Time does strange things when you get older. Sometimes you can't remember last week but sixty years ago is as clear as yesterday.'

'Time could hardly get any more strange for me,' Liana laughed.

They both laughed.

'Did you have any children, Anna?'

Yes, I had two and now I have three grandchildren. My son has two boys and my daughter has a girl. She is twelve and she is called Emily after my mother. I'd like you to meet her. She has copper colour hair just like her great-grandmother and you.' Anna smiled, 'Even if the people here knew that Liana is my real name, who would believe that I was named after you? It's a good secret and I've kept it all my life. I'd like to tell my grandaughter now. What do you think?

'I like the idea and I would like to meet her too.'

'She doesn't live in Barrow so we will have to arrange for you both to visit me at the same time. If you get your dad to drive you over, for once you won't have problems getting back!'

A group of people from Barrow walked passed. A large, friendly looking man shouted across.

'Yer'd better get yourself over to Coppernob, Anna, 'cos the bus'll be goin' soon'.

Joe was there, waiting for them. Anna was so pleased to see him again. She put her arms round both children and they looked together at the old engine. Only Coppernob could share their silent memories.

'Memory is a traveller that disregards time,' Anna said.

Chapter 15

Time to Know

THE weather had turned cold and wet again. In the pouring rain Liana had tried to find Miss Wells to ask her if she would like to live in a flat in The Red House basement. The lady on the reception desk at the University had tried to be helpful.

'I'm sorry love, but I cannot give out student's addresses or phone numbers, but if you leave a note, I'll get it to her for you.'

Liana wrote the note and the receptionist gave her an envelope, but she was disappointed and damp as she walked back through the alleyways to The Red House.

At last a day arrived when Liana woke up to the sun streaming into her bedroom, her spirits rose and she knew she would have a good day. Since the Coppernob meeting things had been better between Liana and her father. He had not said very much about the meeting to Liana, but Jenny had told her that the Museum had been buzzing with stories.

'Everyone has been talking about how Dr Emerson's daughter changed the course of the meeting and the future of Coppernob.'

Jenny had said. 'He is really proud of you, Liana. None of us would have been brave enough to stand up and speak. I've told him that and so have plenty of other people.'

Liana felt an even stronger resolve now than she had felt at the meeting. Her father seemed more relaxed and she was just waiting for the best time to get him to talk to her about her mother. She hoped Uncle Adrian had managed to say something about it to him before he left. Liana hadn't had a chance to find out, but she knew Uncle Adrian wanted to help her and would have done his best. She intended to get it right this time, unlike the discussion about Coppernob. She would try and avoid an argument whatever happened, and keep her father talking instead of walking off.

School was different without Miss Wells. The new teacher was so keen on games and drama that their class took any spare time in the hall and had even gone outside to play football in the rain. One day Liana came home from school covered in mud, but she had scored a goal and everyone had cheered. Liana had never even played a football game before and it felt very strange to be asked to join in the practices after school. Now the sun was shining she was sure they would be outside again, so she packed her football things and went down for breakfast.

Time for Coppernob

'There is a letter for you,' Mark Emerson said to his daughter as she sat down with her toast. 'There is a postcard from Uncle Adrian too.'

He handed her the postcard and Liana looked at the picture of green, wooded islands in a bright blue sea. 'It will soon be winter here in New Zealand,' Uncle Adrian had written. 'However often I travel it is always strange to change season so quickly.'

Liana knew this from her travels with Coppernob, but of course she couldn't say anything. Liana looked at her own letter. It was posted in York and as she hoped, it was from Miss Wells. It was quite a long chatty letter, but Liana skimmed over the words looking to see if she wanted the flat. She did, and she wanted to share it with her friend Suzanne, Miss Thompson. Liana was both relieved and delighted and read the important paragraph to her dad:

> *'Thank you very much for thinking of me before you*
> *advertise your basement flat. Please tell your*
> *father that as long as we can afford the rent,*
> *Suzanne and I would love to live in The Red House*
> *Flat. At the moment we are living with separate*
> *friends, but we are both desperate to move out*
> *so we can have some space and peace before our exams.'*

Dr Emerson folded his paper and stood up.

'They can pay the same rent as they did for their previous flat, if that is fair. You can ask them if they would like to come with us to buy the furniture and kitchen things.'

There was a note enclosed for the class so Liana copied down Miss Wells' telephone number and put the letter away in her bag to read again more carefully later.

As she walked home from school that afternoon the sun felt warm. The pavements were drying and the early blossom was coming out. Liana had intended to visit the Museum after school, but now she had a phone call to make. Liana tried to imagine where Miss Wells was living, with her friends. It couldn't be too far from The Red House. It seemed so long before the phone was answered, Liana had almost given up, but just as she decided to put the phone down a man's voice answered and Liana could hear him shouting.

'Helen, the phone.'

Miss Wells said she would be round in two minutes to look at the basement. She sounded so excited that Liana couldn't wait for her to arrive. She got the key for the basement and found a writing pad to make a list of what they would need to buy. When the doorbell rang Liana jumped, despite having been waiting for it.

Miss Wells looked much younger than at school. She was wearing jeans and she looked quite different with her hair not clipped back. They went straight down into the basement and Liana watched intently to see whether she liked it or not. The sun was shining through the windows showing up the dust, but making everywhere light and cheerful.

'It's perfect,' she said, although Liana had already seen how pleased she looked.

'Do you know how much the rent will be?' Miss Wells asked.

'The same as your last flat if that is fair?' Liana watched her smile grow.

'It's a deal. Suzanne will agree, there is no doubt. It is just what we want. I'm hoping she will be here soon. I left a message on her mobile.'

'You will need some furniture. My dad said that perhaps you would like to come with us to choose it? I've brought a pad to make a list.'

'You are certainly a good planner. I think you would make a good teacher.' Miss Wells said laughing.

'I think I had better try and be a good landlady first,' Liana said.

They had just settled down on the beanbags to start the list when the bell went again. Liana let Miss Thompson in and showed her to the basement.

'I'll make you a coffee if you would like one?' Liana called down the stairs.

'Yes, please,' they both answered together.

The sound of their voices discussing the flat made Liana feel really happy. Even if she didn't see them very often it would be good to know they were around.

Time for Coppernob

The buying furniture trip was a great success, and so was the cleaning party when lots of student friends turned up to help clean the flat and eat pizza. The furniture arrived and the flat was soon ready.

'There is only one problem,' Miss Wells (Helen, as she said she wanted to be called) told Liana. 'A kitten has adopted Suzanne and we wondered whether your dad would mind if he lived with us here?'

'I think that would be brilliant,' Liana said. 'I've asked for a cat before. The only reason we didn't get one was because we are out so much of the time. Might we share it?'

'That sounds like a very good idea, perhaps you could think up a good name for him?

'I'd like to call him Rumpels, short for Rumpelstiltskin.'

'I really like that name,' Suzanne said. 'Rumpels will suit him as he likes to jump in the washing basket and rumple the clothes.'

Helen, Suzanne and the kitten settled in quickly. Rumpels claimed as his own the whole house and garden. He was not supposed to sleep in Liana's room, but Rumpels made up his own mind about these things.

Liana phoned Joe to tell him about the kitten and the new tenants in the basement flat.

'I wonder where you got the name Rumpels from?' Joe laughed.

'You did look funny trying to carry that poor old shell-shocked cat. Do you realise that I am the only one who knows you saved the first Rumpels?'

'No you're not,' Liana reminded him, 'Anna will remember too.'

Joe, hardly ever serious about anything, was really pleased to hear that Liana had company in The Red House. He was very impressed that she had played football and scored a goal with her first shot. She had been lucky to catch Joe in the house, as football had taken over his life again. With the better weather he was always out, either playing in a match or practising. As might be expected, he couldn't resist a joke about her goal.

'You have a 100% success Liana, keep this up and you will soon be playing on Wembley turf and commanding a huge fee. I can just imagine your style.' Liana knew what was coming and was laughing before he started his commentary.

'Liana Emerson's superb performance in her debut match kept the watching crowd in wonder. Despite the state of the pitch after the heavy rain, she out manoeuvred three defenders as she cut inside, leaving the centre half standing and beating the goalkeeper with a superbly placed shot.'

'It was not quite like that,' Liana admitted.

'A goal is always a good goal in football, that's the way to win.'

'Is your foot better now?'

'The foot is fine, but the trainers have gone to the happy football pitch in the sky, or maybe I should say the golf course because of the hole in one.'

'You're impossible to talk to on the phone,' Liana told him but he held her attention when he asked her if she had heard about Coppernob.

'I've not been to the Museum just recently,' Liana told him. 'What's happening?'

'Mum says arrangements are being made to take Coppernob back to Barrow for a visit. I'd like to go and see that, wouldn't you? It is time we had another adventure.'

Liana was cross that her dad hadn't mentioned this to her. Joe didn't have any details, but they agreed to find out more and keep in touch.

Liana decided not to question her father about Coppernob just yet. It would take time to arrange the visit to Barrow and Joe wouldn't let them miss anything. First, she must get him to talk to her about her mother. Saturday seemed like a good time as it was his day off work and he would not be so tired. It would also be difficult for him to get out of talking to her for a whole weekend. On Saturday morning Liana heard her dad getting up quite early so she got up too and joined him in the kitchen. Liana helped make the breakfast and she waited until they had finished eating before she spoke.

'We've got to talk about Mum.' Liana took hold of his arm as he started to get up from the table.

'This is not the right time.'

'Why?'

'I've got a number of things to do today, Liana.'

'OK. How about tonight when you have finished your jobs?'

'All right, all right, we will talk, tonight,' he said as he hurried off.

Liana spent the rest of the morning collecting her evidence together. She took out the two photographs she had taken from the boxes when she first looked in the basement. She kept them in a drawer by her bed. Liana had looked at them so often she knew them well. One was of her mum and dad holding hands, looking happy and relaxed. It was sunny and her mother looked young and full of life. She was wearing a light coloured long skirt and a pale blue tee shirt. In her hand she held a floppy straw hat. Her shining, copper hair was just like Liana's. Her dad looked brown from the sun and was laughing at the person taking the photograph.

Liana hoped the other photograph was of her grandparents. She looked at it again and wondered how long ago it had been taken. The garden they were standing in looked neat and well cared for, with many coloured flowers and the bright white picket fence she had noticed when she first saw the picture. Her mum looked comfortable in the middle of the two older people. They were all smiling straight into the camera with their arms around each other. Liana wondered what it might feel like to be hugged by your own grandparents. She remembered Emily finding her grandparents. If only she had grandparents like Grandma Annie and Grandad Ted waiting to find her. What had happened to her family? Would she find out in just a few hours' time?

She opened the shoebox in her wardrobe and found the postcard she thought might be from her grandparents to her mother. Liana studied the four little pictures of Niagara-on-the-Lake. One picture had a garden with a white fence just like the one on the photograph. Liana remembered that she had seen a similar fence at the Canada exhibition on her adventure with Joe and Kaleem in Wembley. She went back downstairs, found the atlas and looked up Niagara. There were seven entries for Niagara, as it seemed to be in both the United States of America and in Canada. The last entry was for Niagara-on-the-Lake and that was definitely Canada. In the corner of the page, the section of the map Liana wanted to look at was enlarged and she could easily see the Niagara River with the United States on one side and Canada on the other. Niagara-on-the-Lake was, just like its name suggested, right on the edge where the Niagara River joined the huge Lake Ontario.

Liana picked up her old woollen rabbit with a French name, Pierre Lapin. Who had given her rabbit this name? Did her mother speak French? Liana felt as though she was trying to put together a jigsaw but as yet there were too many lost pieces to see what the picture would be. Her dad had the missing information, and whatever happened she must get him to tell her tonight. It was the longest Saturday ever. She had just managed to get images of Niagara-on-the-Lake up on the computer when it crashed; it could sense the tension in her fingers. The television became boring and a DVD she had borrowed was sticking and flickering. When a thick white line appeared blocking out the faces Liana switched it off in disgust. She walked across the city to the library and came out without a book. She bought some Smarties and ate them one by one until they had all gone. That evening neither Liana nor her father felt like making food, so they had a Chinese take-away and ate it watching the television. Liana thought she was hungry but soon the food began to stick in her throat. She noticed that her father hadn't eaten all of his either. When he took the dishes out to the kitchen, she turned off the television.

110

15 - Time to Know

Liana placed the postcard, the picture and Pierre the rabbit on the coffee table. Mark Emerson looked at the small collection and then at his daughter.

'I don't know where to start,' he said, picking up the floppy rabbit, which looked so small in his big hands.

'Mum was Canadian, wasn't she?'

'Yes, I thought you knew that?'

'May be. How did you meet her?'

'Your mother, Beth, won a scholarship and came to England to study engineering. Part of her studies involved working on a project with me at the university. We knew we loved each other right from the first time we met. I thought she was very beautiful. She had copper coloured hair just like yours.'

He looked at the photograph of himself and Beth.

'She was friendly, confident and strong willed. We wanted to get married straight away but she was young, quite a bit younger than me and she hadn't finished her studies. She knew her parents would not approve so we got married without telling them. Uncle Adrian took this photograph soon after the wedding. Your mother's parents were so angry when we told them they refused to have anything to do with us. They put down the phone when Beth rang and didn't answer her letters.'

'Did they speak French to one another?' Liana asked.

'Your mother spoke fluent French. She went to a school where she was taught in French rather than just learning the language. She gave Pierre his French name. We both chose Liana as your name because we liked it and it sounded right with Lagrange and Emerson. We were so pleased when we found out later that the name Liana was originally French too. You are right, many people in Canada do speak French, but despite their French name, your mother and her family came from near Toronto where they speak English.'

Liana's father picked up the postcard.

'Beth was your grandparents' only child and they must have been very disappointed when she decided not to go home, but by not keeping in touch they were hurting themselves as well as us. When you were born we hoped that they would relent and forgive her. Eventually they started to write to each other. As you see from the postcard they mention you, but it isn't addressed to me. They blamed me for taking her away from them.'

'Did you go to Canada to make friends?'

'Yes, we decided to go back to try and sort things out between us.'

'Why didn't you take me?'

'We did take you. Your mum hardly went anywhere without you. We thought that once they had seen you, your grandparents would accept us as a family. I think they would have done, but then we had the accident.'

This was difficult for him. Liana guessed that in all the years since, her father had never spoken about the accident. The postcard was shaking in his hand. Liana moved closer to him and took his hand in hers.

'The accident was my fault Liana, but I was not hurt. You were shocked but the hospital couldn't find a cut or a bruise on you. They said that Beth died instantly and would not have felt any pain. Your grandparents would have liked you to stay in Canada with them, but you and I came back home together after the funeral. I have tried to make the life for us that your mother would have wanted. When I got the job at the Museum and we moved to York, I bought The Red House because your mother would have loved this house. It is too big for us really. It feels better now the basement is lived in.'

'I love The Red House too,' Liana said thoughtfully. She was beginning to understand how difficult it must have been for her dad trying to carry on for her sake, to give her the things her mum would have wanted. Picking up the photograph of her mother and her grandparents, Liana looked at her father.

'Would you like to try to contact your grandparents?' he asked.
'I could help you find them. We do need more people in our lives. I used to spend quite a bit of time at Uncle Adrian's house when I was at school. His parents have invited us to go and visit. Would you like to go?'

'I would like to very much, but most of all I would like to find my own grandparents. I did talk to Uncle Adrian about this at Christmas,' Liana confessed.

'I am so glad you did. Adrian told me you had. I have an address where I hope I can contact your grandparents. I will write a letter tonight. I know I should have talked to you more about your mother, but the only way I have managed without her is by hiding my feelings. I am sorry, Liana.'

Liana couldn't bear to see her father's eyes full of sorrow and regret. She buried her head in his chest and they hugged and comforted each other for their loss. Mark Emerson stroked his daughter's hair and told her how afraid he was of losing her love, especially now she was growing up so quickly.

'I have been planning a surprise for you and your friend Joe,' he told her. 'Coppernob is going back to Barrow. I thought you might like to go over to see her displayed there.'

'Could we invite Joe's mum and his brother to come too, they don't have a car so it would be difficult for them to get there?' Liana asked.

'Of course, the more the merrier.'

That didn't sound one bit like her father speaking. Liana felt the sadness lifting. He really did mean what he said.

Chapter 16

The Right Time

JOE arrived at the Museum before Liana on Thursday evening. He was already hard at work cleaning Coppernob when she arrived.

'Come on,' he called down from the top of the boiler. 'I will have done all the work if you don't get started soon.'

'I know,' Liana shouted back, 'it takes one and a half hours just to polish the copper firebox dome.'

'Where ever did you get information like that, Liana Emerson?' he asked, grinning and shaking his head. The Museum was closed and Joe and Liana had been allowed to help get Coppernob ready to go back to Barrow. It really was strange to be cleaning her again.

'You have been through the wars a bit it seems,' Joe said, as he wiped round the scars carefully. The children smiled at each other when one of the engineers, greasing and oiling the wheels, tried to explain to them that the holes in Coppernob really were caused by shrapnel damage during the war.

'It must have been very bad in Barrow to cause this much damage,' he continued.

'Coppernob was lucky really. It could have been much worse,' Joe said, but a look from Liana stopped him saying any more.

'It is a pity she can no longer be in steam,' a volunteer polisher added.

'She has already done more than enough work for one engine,' Joe replied protectively.

Everyone polished until their backs and shoulders ached from rubbing and buffing and Coppernob shone. They stood back to admire their work. There was no way they could cover up Coppernob's dents and rips but the paint looked so bright and the brass and copper gleamed.

'You can be proud to go home, Coppernob,' Liana said quietly. She wished that Grandad Ted could see his engine now. Joe must have been thinking the same thing as he whispered in her ear.

'I think there is a happy old engine driver looking down from wherever old engine drivers go when they die, "She polishes up well this old girl", he is saying.'

Coppernob was due to be transported back to Barrow-in-Furness leaving at 10.00 a.m. the next day, which was a Friday, a school day. Liana really wanted to be there, but she thought her father would not agree to her taking time off school, not even for Coppernob. She wished she had asked him when he told

her he had made plans with Joe's mum to visit Barrow on the Saturday. He had seemed to be really looking forward to the trip and Liana had not wanted to spoil the moment.

'We will have to leave early to get there in time for Coppernob's homecoming celebrations,' he had told her. He even thought it was a good idea to phone Anna to make arrangements to meet. Liana had felt so much more content since they had talked about her mother. She didn't want anything to spoil her new relationship with her dad.

As her thoughts could only be with Coppernob, Liana reasoned to herself, there would be no point being in school on Friday morning. Joe had no such worries. He was going to see Coppernob travelling through York, whatever happened.

'This will be a once in a life time experience,' he told her. 'And after all, if it wasn't for you, Coppernob would not be going at all. You deserve to see her if anyone does. Have you never heard the saying, "Rules are for the obedience of the stupid and the guidance of the wise". More importantly, if you obey

16 - The Right Time

all the rules you miss all the fun. Seeing Coppernob set off on her journey to Barrow will be an education in itself.'

He would have continued, but Liana stopped him.

'All right,' she said, 'I'm thinking about it.'

Joe had noticed a table being set up, not far away, with delicious looking 'help yourself' food. The Museum was often used for meetings and parties and Joe had seen tables set up before, but this was the first time he had seen the food arrive.

'Look at all that food over there,' Joe wiped his hands on his tee-shirt 'I'm really hungry now, aren't you?'

Liana was starving, but she had seen her dad and a small group of people heading towards them.

'Let me introduce you to the volunteers who have been cleaning Coppernob before her journey,' Dr Emerson said to the engineers from Barrow. The grown-ups started shaking hands and talking. A tall gentleman, Liana recognised as the leader of the Barrow engineers looking after Coppernob, came up to her and handed her an envelope.

'The Furness Railway Trust would like to show you their appreciation,' he said. 'We always thought it would be too much responsibility to have Coppernob permanently in Barrow. We are however delighted that she is coming home for a visit. We would like you to accept a complimentary family ticket for the Lakeside and Haverthwaite Railway, to ride behind 'The Great Survivor', Furness engine No 20.'

He explained that, having rebuilt her, she was now the oldest working engine in the country.

'No 20 is the nearest you could get to riding behind Coppernob herself,' he added.

Liana thanked him and had no difficulty finding the courage to ask if her family could include Joe, his mum and his brother.

'Of course, you are all very welcome,' he said. 'I will send you a timetable but if you can manage a Tuesday we all dress up as Victorians. We hope to see you all at Haverthwaite Station. After all your hard work, we shall have to make a special effort if No 20 is to look as bright and well cared for as Coppernob.'

'Coppernob does look magnificent,' Mark Emerson said, and turning towards the children he added, 'I do hope all your efforts cleaning and polishing have given you an appetite, and you will help us eat all this food.'

Joe would have been the first there, but the other volunteers went to wash their hands first so he felt he ought to go too. Joe's mother and his brother Peter had been invited to the meal, and soon there was plenty of excited chatter as they discussed the plans for Coppernob's journey the following day.

'Would you two be able to get up really early tomorrow?' Liana's dad said, looking at his daughter and Joe. 'We start moving Coppernob at 7-30 a.m. and I am sure you wouldn't want to miss anything.'

Liana was just about to say something about school when Joe kicked her, and instead she said, 'Of course we will both be here really early. We must be here from the start.'

The light was fading as Liana and her dad walked home through York to The Red House.

'Thank you for letting me see Coppernob go off on her journey to Barrow tomorrow,' Liana said, putting her arm through her dad's arm and holding on tight.

'You deserve it. You were very brave at the Coppernob meeting. We were all so sure we were right but you and Anna could see a compromise and now we are all happy with the outcome. I am so proud of you. I find it hard to say these things but I mean it, Liana.'

Liana rested her head on his arm. She was tired and sleepy and happier than she could remember.

It was half-light when the alarm went off. For a moment Liana felt confused and uncertain about what was happening. She was not used to getting up this early, but as soon as she remembered Coppernob, she got out of bed and went through the motions of getting washed and dressed without really thinking what she was doing. Across the other side of York, Joe could not be woken. He had eaten too much and gone to bed too late the night before. His mother shook him but the muscles in his arm hurt and he complained bitterly.

'Peter and I will say goodbye to Coppernob for you,' his mother warned. 'I'll tell Liana you wouldn't get out of bed.'

That did it. He crawled out of bed, put on his clothes and sullenly ate his Crunchy Nut Cornflakes and toast.

The early morning sunlight poured through the windows in the Museum roof, lighting Coppernob as she waited to take part in the adventures of the day. The engine 'Gladstone' had already been moved off the turntable by the time Liana and Joe arrived. The rails leading to the huge glass doors were empty and waiting for Coppernob. All went well - at first.

'How will we get Coppernob on to the turntable?' Liana asked her dad.

'The pig will push her,' he replied, smiling, for the first and last time that morning, at the puzzled look on Liana's face.

Before Liana could respond he had joined two men positioning a strange machine, behind Coppernob. This was the pig.

'It looks more like a cross between a hand held plough and a mowing machine than a pig.' Joe had to shout to Liana over the noise the pig had suddenly started making. The noise came from its little engine. It had two handles, but instead of blades it had a pusher at the front and a rubber wheel to grip the floor. Dr Emerson was in charge, checking that Coppernob was properly oiled before removing the chocks and giving the signal to push. The procedure was being watched carefully by the small group from Barrow-in-Furness. They had, after much searching, found a transporter low enough to carry Coppernob under the Leeman Road railway bridge just outside the Museum. They were now eager to have their engine and take her back to Barrow.

Coppernob rolled smoothly on to the turntable. When she was secure the turntable was moved sedately round so that Coppernob could be pushed towards the huge glass doors and out to freedom. So far so good, Liana enjoyed seeing her beautiful old friend back on the turntable in the middle of all the other engines, where she belonged. It seemed such a long time ago since she had written her poem for the infants. Even Joe was watching quietly as, with a little help from the pig, Coppernob's pistons moved and her wheels went round. Just as if under her own steam, the elegant old engine rolled out of the Museum and into the bright sunshine, ready for her journey home. From then on it looked as though Coppernob had decided not to go!

First of all her low-slung ash-pan smashed into the transporter.

Everyone, except the driver, rushed to see if Coppernob was damaged. The driver rushed to check his low loader. The end of the transporter was badly dented but Coppernob, thank goodness, was fine. Slowly and gradually, Coppernob began the haul up the ramp. Everyone watched and held their breath as Coppernob crept slowly up the incline. Then, a loud gasping sound came from the anxious onlookers as Coppernob toppled precariously and derailed. The engineers swarmed onto the low loader shouting instructions. They put in the jacks and gently levered her back on the tracks.

'Maybe it feels like an insult to be loaded onto a lorry,' Liana whispered to Joe.

'According to Grandad Ted she did this when she was unloaded from the ship at Barrow Docks,' Joe reminded Liana.

'Steady on now, old girl,' the chief engineer from Barrow said, talking to Coppernob as if she was a horse, in just the same way as the 7th Duke of Devonshire had so many years ago. Gradually they eased her along and into place, securing her and checking until everyone was satisfied. After a brief shaking of hands, Coppernob was handed over to the Barrow engineers. The low loader revved up and pulled slowly away from the Museum. Coppernob slid with just enough room for safety under the long, low bridge at Leeman Road. Joe and Liana followed behind the transporter, running to keep up as it gathered speed under the bridge and disappeared round the bend in the road.

'It has to turn left, go under the city walls and come back round so we will see her again if we keep running,' Joe called to Liana.

As they came out from the darkness of the bridge and into the light, they could see that Coppernob was not going anywhere for the moment. The driver, deciding to avoid going under the walls, had tried to turn right against the flow of traffic in a one-way section. Everyone on the road had come to a halt. Horns were blowing and people were getting out of their cars to look. Coppernob towered above it all with her chimney high in the air, as defiant as ever. It took some time before the police, on motorcycles, were able to get through the traffic hold-up to guide Coppernob out of York and untangle the jammed streets throughout the city. Coppernob created her own dramatic exit from York, but her arrival in Barrow was greeted by huge, waiting crowds delighted to have their engine home.

16 - The Right Time

The car journey to Barrow-in-Furness, the next day, seemed to take forever. It felt strange to Liana to have the car full of people. Joe's mum had brought so much food they could have eaten all day. Liana sat in between Peter and Joe in the back. For the first time she could really imagine what it would be like to have a family with a mother and brothers. It was quiet when they set off as everyone was sleepy from getting up early two days in a row, but by the time they were nearing Barrow even Peter was talking. Liana had never known such a noisy journey. She couldn't really hear what her dad and Joe's mum were saying to each other, but they laughed a lot.

They had one stop on the journey when Joe noticed a signpost for Clapham and remembered that Coppernob had been to Clapham. They did a quick detour to look at the station and stretch their legs, but Liana's dad explained that Coppernob had visited a different, much bigger Clapham in London. Liana gave Joe a look and he kept very quiet about Wembley. He was not so careful, however, when they passed by the sign for the Lakeside and Haverthwaite Railway. The parents were considering dates to use Liana's ticket to ride behind No 20. It was when Joe's mum was persuading Liana's dad that they should all go dressed up as Victorians that Joe got a bit excited.

'If you've never experienced rocking on the footplate of an old steam engine with the pistons pumping and the wind in your face, you have never lived.'

Everyone stopped. Liana cringed.

'You sound as if you have actually done this already,' Peter said, looking across Liana, at his brother.

'He has always had a vivid imagination,' their mum joined in from the front. Liana thought it was a good job they were in the car in case her face gave something away. Joe, on the other hand, played it along as would be expected. He handed round a large packet of wine gums he'd bought, when they stopped for petrol. The plastic bag ripped and the three of them were kept busy looking for the lost wine gums before the warmth in the car made the sweets hot and sticky.

All was quiet again in the car as they pulled into Barrow Railway Station. Joe and Liana were shocked to see that the rebuilt station looked like a cardboard box. They had seen for themselves the destruction of the old station with its beautiful curving glass and timber roof, but both of them had somehow expected it to still be there. The low loader had been parked so that Coppernob, still firmly attached, was resting in exactly the same place as she had done for all those years in her elegant glass case. Coppernob was surrounded by Barrow-in-Furness people once more. Barrow-in-Furness was bright with little flags flapping in the warm breeze. There were flowers and posters for the Coppernob homecoming festivities everywhere. The station car park had been turned into an arena and people had already begun to take their seats for the opening ceremony.

'Look,' Joe shouted to Liana, pointing out an older lady sitting talking, close to Coppernob. 'It's Anna.'

Liana caught her breath, mistakenly thinking that she could see the young Emily with her, but realising almost immediately that this must be Anna's grandaughter, also called Emily and named after her great -grandmother. The two children made their way through the crowd towards them. As Mark Emerson watched his daughter hug the old lady, he wondered whether Liana's own grandparents would reply to his letter. He desperately hoped they would.

The ceremony began with the Ulverston town band playing a tune called 'Will Ye No Come Back Again', beneath a sign, which read:

'WELCOME HOME FURNESS'S LONG LOST HERO.'

There were speeches and three cheers for Coppernob before the festivities were eventually declared open. Many memories were stirred and quiet tears shed. Young children were lifted high to see the shining dome. Older people were helped to the front so that they could touch their old engine one more time. An old man in a wheelchair patted Coppernob gently with a wrinkled brown hand.

'I used to meet my wife, God rest her soul, right here by Coppernob in her glass case. That was when I was a young man,' he said in a soft, misty voice. 'I think about those times a lot now.' He took out his handkerchief and blew loudly. 'I never thought I would ever see Coppernob again.' His voice trailed off and he was lost in his thoughts.

So many events had been arranged in honour of Coppernob's return it was difficult to decide what to do first. Liana's dad had things to discuss with the tall man from the Furness Railway Trust, who had given Liana the Lakeside and Haverthwaite ticket. Peter and Joe wanted to go to the fun fair whereas their mother preferred the craft fair. They all agreed to meet up again, by Coppernob, in two hours. This gave Liana time to talk to Anna and to get to know Emily her grandaughter.

'You two could be sisters, you look so alike with your copper coloured hair,' Anna said, as they walked back over the road bridge to Chadwick Street.

'Grandma has told me all about you meeting my great-grandmother, the one I am named after. It is such an amazing story.'

'Sometimes I can hardly believe it myself,' Liana said, looking through the railway fencing where the long brick wall used to be.

'I remember the signal box just here, where I met the first Emily's father.' She shivered at the thought. 'He was frightening but her Grandfather Ted and Grandma Annie were the loveliest people I've ever met.'

16 - The Right Time

The last time Liana had been in Chadwick Street, it had just been bombed. At first it all looked exactly back to normal until they reached number 26 and Liana looked above the door where the bomb had landed. She saw that the arch of bricks had been replaced but not the decorative turrets still on all the other houses. Anna laughed when Liana pointed this out.

'We were lucky to get the brick-work done and to be allowed back into our house,' Anna told them. 'Nobody bothered about fancy decoration during the war.'

Inside the house Liana saw that once again the furniture had changed, although the picture of Coppernob and Grandad Ted was back above the fireplace. She was also pleased to see a new collection of teapots now safely housed in a glass-fronted case. Emily listened whilst her grandma and Liana talked about Coppernob, the meeting and many other things they remembered, until Anna became tired.

'I have a gift for both of you,' Anna said, as she handed them each a big, rectangular brown paper parcel. The presents were unwrapped carefully. Inside they found a perfect copy of the picture above the fireplace with Ted Matthews on his engine, Coppernob. Both girls were delighted and Anna was hugged. There was one more to be given to Joe. All the pictures would be treasured forever. Liana and Emily knew they would always keep in touch. That was what Anna wanted.

'There are some flowers here to take up to the cemetery. Would you two like to take them for me?' Anna asked.

It was a lovely day, windy and sunny just like the last time Liana had walked up the hill to the cemetery with the first Emily. Anna had been just a tiny baby in her pram. You could not see that there had been a war. The damaged houses had been re-built and the red bricks were bright and clean, each house with a different front door now. The school had gone and a new church had been built, but the old church hall was still there. Over the door they read a notice with old-fashioned spellings:

LICENSED IN PUSUENCE OF THE ACTS OF PARLIMENT FOR PUBLIC DANCING, SINGING AND OTHER ENTERTAINMENTS OF LIKE AND KIND

'This is a strange way of saying things,' Emily laughed.

'They used to use different words and say things in different ways then,' Liana explained. 'It is amazing how much has changed and yet so many things have stayed the same. There was no singing and dancing when I was here last. I struggled to carry a very heavy, shell -shocked cat up this hill.'

There were so many flowers placed in the cemetery it looked as if they were growing. They stopped for a moment to get their breath. The air smelt fresh as they looked over the field of flowers and the slate roof tops to the sea. Liana could see changes. Most of the cranes and chimneys were gone and so were the steam trains, all except one, Coppernob, far below behind the houses. The Matthews' family grave was well kept as it always had been. Liana read the new names and dates on the stones and the inscription Grandad Ted had chosen:

: BE-YE-KIND-ONE-TO-ANOTHER : TENDERHEARTED :

She watched Emily remove the old flowers and replace them with the new, just like her great-grandmother had done before her. Liana knew now that her own mother was buried in Canada. One day, she would put flowers on her grave.

Chapter 17

In Just a Short Time

JENNY looked up and smiled as Liana walked into the Museum. She always noticed Liana, however busy she was welcoming visitors and giving them their tickets.

'Shall I let him know that you're here?' she asked.

Liana nodded and smiled back. It was Saturday and Liana knew that in a few minutes her dad would finish his meeting and be free. Automatically, Liana walked through the Main Hall to Coppernob, passing the little yellow signal box on the way. Coppernob was safely back in the Museum after her journey to Barrow. The old engine looked peaceful, bathed in a soft, golden light. Liana rested her head against Coppernob's wheel.

'You've visited your family, Coppernob. Wish with me that I will be able to visit mine.' As she walked round to the front of the engine, Liana trailed her left hand over the sand box lid, the buffers and the beautiful brass number 3. Once again her right hand was in her pocket, holding tightly onto a letter.

A small packet had arrived that morning after her dad had left for work. Even though it was addressed to her, Liana hesitated to open it. She looked at the stamp and the postmark. It was from Canada. What if it was not what she was hoping for so much? She turned it over in her hands but the suspense and the fear were equally unbearable. She opened it. Inside was a packet of sweets called Gummy Bears, a photograph and a letter. Liana looked at the photograph. There, standing by a lake, were the same two people as on the photograph with her mother. They had grey hair now but they looked sun-tanned and smiling. They didn't look really old. Liana turned the photograph over. On the back was written, 'With love to Liana from Grandma and Grandpa'. Liana unfolded the letter and read:

Dear Liana

We were so pleased to hear from Mark and to know that you are well. We were surprised to see your photograph taken by York Minster in the snow. We had not realised that you would look so grown up. The photograph enclosed shows our little dog, Purdy. You would like each other, for sure. We are both sad that we have missed seeing you but we want you to know that we have thought about you often.

Time for Coppernob

*We have recently retired from work and we are moving
to a little house close by where the Niagara river
flows into Lake Ontario. Across the river we can
see America. It is very beautiful here, just like York.
We get lots of visitors in the summer too.
We hope that your dad will bring you to Niagara-
on-the-Lake to visit us. You will both be very
welcome.*

*With love,
Grandma and Grandpa*

Liana read the letter several times before putting it in her pocket and looking again at the photograph. Even the little white dog looked happy and friendly. She had kept her hand on the letter and the photograph all the way to the Museum.

'Hello Liana, I thought I'd find you with Coppernob.' Mark Emerson made his daughter jump. 'Are you all right?' he asked her.

'Yes, I was just thinking,' she replied. 'I've had a letter from Grandma and Grandpa. You didn't say you had sent them a photograph of me.' She handed him the letter and he read it carefully.

'It looks as if it was a good idea though, doesn't it?' he said, giving her a hug and taking the photograph she was showing him.

'Could we?' Liana began but couldn't continue for the tightness gripping her throat. Sitting down on Coppernob's buffer Mark put his arms around his daughter.

'I think it is about time we sent Uncle Adrian a postcard from somewhere exciting don't you?'

'Could it be Canada, Dad?' she managed to ask.

'Canada sounds like a good idea to me. We could collect some brochures from the travel agent on our way home. By the way, this old girl is going back on the turntable for a while.' Mark Emerson patted Coppernob affectionately.

Liana was pleased, although it would not be easy to touch Coppernob on the turntable and it could be difficult if there was another adventure. She didn't say any of that to her dad, of course. Coppernob belonged on the turntable.

When she got home Liana knocked on the basement door. Helen answered and invited her in. The flat looked lovely now with pictures on the walls and lots of lamps and books. Liana showed her the letter and photograph and Suzanne made them all a drink.

'Will you be able to visit your mother's grave?' Helen asked.

Liana felt sure that she would.

'I think it would be good for your dad to go too,' Suzanne joined in from the kitchen. Rumpels wound himself around Liana's legs and purred. They talked for a while whilst they drank their coffee.

'Would you like a gingerbread person?' Suzanne handed them round. 'They're from Thomas the Bakers in Harrogate.'

Liana picked up the familiar little shape.

'It's amazing where they get to,' she said.

Rumpels followed Liana back upstairs and stuck his nose in the packet of sweets from Canada. Liana had a closer look. They were brightly coloured fruit gums in the shape of little bears. She thought of Joe, he would like these. She tried his home number.

'Hello, it's Liana, could I speak to Joe please?' Joe's mum sounded pleased to hear her and chatted about the trip to Barrow whilst she looked round the house for Joe and handed him the phone. Before Liana could speak, however, Joe began talking about their visit to Lakeside and Haverthwaite.

'I know exactly which bit of the Furness Railway it is now,' he told her, in his usual enthusiastic way. 'And, Liana,' he continued before she could get her word in. 'I picked up a pamphlet in Barrow for Holker Hall, where the 7th Duke of Devonshire lived. It is open to the public, so we could go and see where he lived.'

Joe's mum had tried to tell him that there were no amusements at Holker

17 - In Just a Short Time

Hall, but he was still so keen to go. She just couldn't imagine why. Liana could, of course.

Eventually, Liana managed to tell Joe she had something to say to him.

'What's up then?' he asked, cheerful as always.

'I've heard from my grandparents in Canada.'

Joe listened whilst Liana explained about the photograph with the dog.

'You'd like the Gummy Bears, Joe. I've never seen them here.'

'Gummy Bears,' Joe was quiet for a second. 'I think they must be sweets for grandparents with no teeth.'

Liana laughed. She understood his sense of humour now but she felt so happy, she would have laughed at anything.

'Don't eat them all Liana, I need to taste a few for my research,' Joe reminded her as they put the phones down.

Liana felt content but excited too. She slipped a Gummy Bear into her mouth and enjoyed the soft, sweet taste and the smooth surface on her tongue. Her own grandparents had sent her sweets and soon she would be with them. She wondered if, in Canada, they could see the rabbit in the moon that Grandad Ted had shown her. Perhaps she could show them. In just a short time she would know more about her mother and herself. She wanted to shout, to jump and run as fast as she could. She looked at the travel agent's brochures. Any flight would be perfect.